Print books

Jim Nash

Jim Nash The Beginning
Gun Crazy
Gun Crazy 2
Gun Crazy 3
Fallen Angels
Last Stop to Nowhere
Revenge is Justice
Escape / Forget Me Not
Wedding Bell Blues / Breakdown
Mexico Time
No Free Ride / Gone
LOBO
Stealing America
Blame It on Djibouti
No Escape
Trouble in Paradise
Nash & Delaney Collide

Harry Delaney Adventures

Dead Reckoning
Lie Cheat Steal
Uncharted
Go-Around
Sand Storm
Harry Delaney Collection

Frank Ross Biker Tales

No Way Out
Bad Girls
Bank Robber Dames

Other

The Last President

Jim Nash Read Order

JIM NASH

Jim Nash The Beginning
Pirate Cay
Thrill Kill Jill
Greetings From Key West
Lost Paradise
No Angels
Mexico Gamble
No Picnic
Fallen Angels
Vendetta
A Girl's Best Friend
Dead End
No Harbor
Dog Days
Startup Blues
Last Stop To Nowhere / The Last
Goodbye
Revenge Is Justice
Escape
Wedding Bell Blues
Snap Brim Fedora Caper
Breakdown
Little Girl Lost
Forget Me Not
All The Glitter
Mexico Time
Partners In Crime
Shop Till You Drop
Lobo
No Free Ride
Gone
Stealing America
Blame It on Djibouti
No Escape
Trouble in Paradise
Nash & Delaney Collide

SEASONAL

Trick or Treat
Helping Santa

JIM NASH INVESTIGATES

The Snap Brim Fedora Caper
The Lady in White
The Lady in Yellow

WEDDING BELL BLUES

PX DUKE

JIM NASH

WEDDING BELL BLUES

ONE

I was sitting on a bench on the street below my office, relaxing with Maddie Spence, my partner in crime, and her good dog, Friday. A cool breeze floated down the street, a welcome relief from the long hot spell. It was what brought us out with so many others to enjoy the cool evening. Couples paraded past holding hands. Some walked dogs.

The breeze fluttered umbrellas along the row of sidewalk cafés. A strand of Maddie's hair escaped from behind an ear. I reached to tuck it back before replacing my hand to cover hers on the bench between us.

The sun was beginning to descend beneath the buildings on the opposite side of the street. They took on an odd hue, with half the street in dark shade and the other half still in bright daylight.

Friday plopped himself between us at our feet. His tail slowly swished the sidewalk, back and forth and back again, in slow, lazy sweeps. His head swiveled, following people dog-walking their pets past his domain in front of the building.

"Do you think he intends to come between us?" I asked Maddie.

Maddie looked down at the dog sitting between our

legs, separating us. "No, I think Friday has more of a *Let's see what this guy is up to,* kind of wariness."

"Well, he ought to know by now. He's been waking up at the foot of our bed while I'm still in it."

I absently reached to scratch Friday's ear. I was wanting to ask before this, but I didn't think it was any of my business. Now that Maddie was in my life and a part of the business, I decided to go full steam ahead. "When was the last time you had Friday in for a checkup with a veterinarian?" I asked her.

Maddie regarded me with her own wariness. "Are you thinking volunteering for vet payments will give you a percentage ownership in my intended?"

"If your intended is a dog, I'm beginning to have concerns of my own. I'll call tomorrow," I told her.

"In that case, come upstairs and I'll make an attempt at alleviating some of those concerns."

"One at a time, is it?" I asked, with a smile.

"We'll see."

I didn't mind following Maddie anywhere, this or any night. She looked too good in the cutoffs for me to want to take the lead. As though in agreement, Friday woofed and followed behind us as we hurried up the two flights of stairs.

Maddie's giggle turned uncontrollable by the time we reached the top step to the apartment above the office. Friday hesitated outside the door, as though already having enough of our silliness.

I called to the dog, but it was Maddie's hand signal that convinced the animal to enter behind us.

"Good boy, Friday. You can guard the door."

Disgusted with his mistress and her happy-go-lucky attitude to the other male in her life, Friday headed off to his plush bed in the living room. Maddie and I made for our own plush king-size bed.

Friday woofed his disapproval as the giggling

quieted and more earnest sounds assaulted his delicate doggie ears.

I t was late morning when we chased each other into the kitchen. By then, the entire building had cooled, thanks to the change in the weather.

"Are you going to call the veterinarian, or am I?" Maddie asked.

I was glad Maddie brought it up. Friday was her dog, after all. "I know one we can walk to. I did some work for her a couple of years ago."

"Her?" Maddie's hands went to her hips as she regarded me.

"She's happily married, don't worry," I insisted.

"I wasn't worried about her."

"You needn't be concerned about me, either. I'm thrilled to be involved with my partner. And her dog. In case you haven't noticed."

"Well, I have to admit, I've been wondering if it was more about Friday than me," she said.

I turned off the stove. Breakfast would go cold. I picked up a grinning Maddie and hauled the woman off, feet kicking, to the bedroom. "Let's see if I can wipe that smile off your face."

"If this is how you're planning on doing it, I'd bet money you're going to be a failure," she assured me.

I dropped her on the bed. "We'll just have to see about that, won't we?"

A n uneasy Friday looked from Maddie to Jim and back again. He appeared anxious about the upcoming walk without his mistress, especially on hearing the unfamiliar word over and over.

"It's all good, Friday. Jim loves you, too. Not as much

as I do, but he's learning."

Jim flipped a look Maddie's way and attached Friday's leash. She walked with them downstairs to street level, like an anxious parent on a child's first day.

"All right. We're on our way to the vet. Text us if you need us."

Friday's ears perked up. There it was again, that word he didn't know.

Maddie waved, and Friday's tail wagged. The pair started out with Friday testing Jim. He walked ahead, tugging at the confines of the leash. Jim called *Heel,* and the dog obeyed instantly. Maddie was secretly pleased that Jim was making her dog obey. She was even more pleased that Friday paid attention. It meant he was accepting Jim into his life.

She returned to the second-floor office and killed time checking texts and voice mail and email. It kept her from worrying about Friday's encounter with the veterinarian. It had never occurred to her to take the otherwise healthy dog to a vet.

She printed out an email to Jim about a wedding invitation. She saved a voice mail from a Warren-someone who wanted Jim to call him.

The email intrigued her. It expressed concern about why there hadn't been an RSVP to confirm he was coming to the wedding. She checked the date and circled the day on Jim's desk calendar. She considered buying a new dress or two on the off chance she would be invited as Jim's plus one.

She thought some more and knew there would be no *off chance*. If Jim was going to a wedding, she'd darn well be going with him, invitation or not. Already she was going through a list of what she would have to buy. She'd be darned if she would show up with a backpack full of wrinkled clothes.

Maddie tapped the space bar on the office laptop to

bring it to life. She began a search for a new suitcase. It wouldn't arrive in time. She would have to buy local once she knew what she wanted.

She was busy thinking about color and size options when the phone rang.

TWO

The **walk to** Dr. Hannah's clinic was twenty minutes, maybe thirty. I didn't mind. Neither did Friday. It was good exercise for both of us, and something I needed. I allowed him to get out of sight of his mistress and then gave him the lead to prance along at his own pace. He wandered and sniffed and snuffled and checked out the unfamiliar smells on the way to Hannah's.

A few years ago, I did some work with Dr. Hannah. Someone was stealing pets from wealthy owners. The thieves ended up blackmailing the owners into paying a ransom to get them back.

"Here we are, Friday. It's a new place for both of us." Well, okay, it wasn't new for me, but a dog wouldn't know that.

Friday wasn't so keen on entering the strange building with the antiseptic smells all around him. He hesitated and halted at every door, testing the air with a wet nose before slowly walking in. He relented at the sound of Hannah's soothing voice.

She smiled a greeting at me and addressed the dog with a practiced enthusiasm. "This must be Friday. I'm Hannah. Hello Friday. Aren't you a handsome boy."

That got Friday's attention. She stroked the dog's

neck and scratched his ear. Friday looked from me to her and suddenly I was on doggie ignore. Hanna patted the table and Friday pranced up the steps and sat down without a care in the world.

As far as I was concerned, Friday was enjoying the attention far too much. He preened and showed great patience as Dr. Hannah felt and probed and examined and pressed. She made sure to talk to him the entire time. When it was all done, it was a tossup who was more exhausted by all the attention, Friday or me.

He behaved well, and Hannah was impressed. The last thing she did was run a scanner between Friday's shoulder blades before entering the data into her laptop. "Well now. That's strange." She looked from Friday to me and back to her laptop.

"What's wrong? Is he okay? He's not sick, is he?" I dreaded returning to Maddie with the news.

"Oh no. Friday is in excellent health. Maybe a bit overweight, but nothing serious. You should make sure he gets exercise."

It wouldn't hurt either of us, but I didn't say anything.

"Do you recall the RFID chips in those stolen dogs we worked on?" Dr. Hannah asked. "We used them to locate the owners."

"Yes. I remember." Almost all the stolen pets had microchip implants. The device, about the size of a grain of rice, was injected between the shoulder blades, much like a vaccination. The RFID remained in place for the life of the pet. Each chip had a unique identification code, which was registered to a database listing the owners. It was how we ended up returning the animals to their rightful owners.

"Friday has one. His code comes back linked to someone named Lily Sands. Do you know anything about that?"

"I know a Lily Sands. She's the daughter of a friend of mine out on the panhandle. Panama Crossing."

"Yes, well, that's the address linked to your dog. And his name is Max."

I didn't explain that Friday wasn't my dog. I didn't tell Dr. Hannah about Maddie, either. Or that Friday was her dog. Except now, Friday wasn't Maddie's dog.

Friday was Lily's dog, and his name was Max.

C aller ID would tell Maddie it was me. I knew she was concerned about having Friday at the veterinarian's, too, and she picked up before the first ring halted. "I'm just checking in. We're still with Dr. Hannah. Do you remember when you last took Friday for a visit to a veterinarian?" I thought I'd start out slow.

"I've never had him for a checkup. Friday has never been ill. I never even thought about it. Is he all right? He's not sick, is he?" Maddie cleared her throat attempting to hide a voice shaky with emotion. I recognized her concern immediately.

"I'm putting you on speaker with Dr. Hannah.

"Friday is fine. He's healthy as a dog. Maybe a little pudgy for his age."

"Well, I know someone else—"

I had to interrupt her. "No, Maddie. You're perfect just the way you are." I knew before my mouth closed it was the wrong thing to say.

Hannah regarded me with raised eyebrows before wagging a finger and shaking her head for good measure. Maddie didn't let the unseen interrupt her.

"I was talking about you, shamus. Maybe I should put the pair of you on a strict diet and exercise plan if you're taking us to a wedding."

"A wedding?" Damn. How did she find out? I hadn't told her about Allie's wedding. Or anything about Allie.

My plan was to ignore the whole thing. I didn't think anyone would be missing me.

"You can read all about it when you get back."

Maddie hung up, and it left me to my own devices to clear up inconsistencies in Friday's past with the veterinarian's help. "I don't know how long Maddie and Friday have been together. I'm pretty sure she wouldn't just up and take him. She has to have found him somewhere."

"Well, the implant doesn't lie. He's definitely one from the litter. The information and the address are plain as day. Does she have any records?"

I thought briefly. "Not that I know, but I never asked. I just assumed she owned the dog. She must have spent a lot of time training him. He obeys every one of her signals. She even gives them to him when she knows he won't obey me. She thinks I don't know."

"By the sound of it they have a good rapport. I doubt they'd be so close if they didn't. Perhaps a previous owner beat Friday."

"Oh no. I don't believe that for a minute. Although, now that you mention it, there are times I could put that woman over my knee."

"You do have a way with words, don't you, James?" Dr. Hannah admonished him. "I'd bet if Maddie were here now, you'd be eating them."

I grinned at Dr. Hannah. "I wouldn't be saying them. You know me by now."

Dr. Hannah went on. "Maybe a previous owner didn't do notifications on the change of ownership. That happens sometimes. The new owner doesn't know, and the previous doesn't bother."

"All right. Well, in that case, I have a phone call to make. Someone is going to be thrilled to learn their lost dog has been found." I didn't tell her Maddie was definitely not going to be happy about it.

Hannah said her goodbyes to Friday and told him he could come back anytime. Friday only snorted at the indignity of the standing invitation and pulled me to the door, anxious to be getting home. I allowed him to tug at his leash all the way. He was obviously rushing to put the strange scents in Dr. Hannah's office as far behind as he could. He trotted eagerly, anticipating treats and the petting and the scratching. I didn't call him to heel.

I was preoccupied with the reaction Maddie was about to have. She definitely would not be happy to find out the main squeeze in her life was someone's lost dog now found.

THREE

I tried to make the news about Friday and her owner as easy for Maddie as I could. It wasn't going well. She was despondent. I knew she would be. Immediately, she backed away and crossed her arms, refusing to listen. I had betrayed her. She could hardly look at me. She swallowed so hard I could hear it.

"Maybe I sort of suspected when I found him waiting for me by the car door. I was at a rest stop. I opened the door, and he volunteered to jump in. I knew he must belong to someone. We sort of adopted each other. He didn't look mistreated. I checked him over very carefully. He didn't have a collar. Or maybe he lost it somewhere. I never thought to check for one of those tags. I didn't know about them."

Maddie's explanation came out too short and clipped to be a lie.

"I believe you. You love Friday. That was plain as day from the first time I saw you with him." Hell, even I thought the two of them belonged together from day one. They were a Mutt and Maddie of dog and human.

"What are you going to do?" she wanted to know.

"I don't know, Maddie, but I do know a young person who is very concerned about the welfare of her dog."

She wasn't having it. "Well, I need a break. We're off to the beach to think about things. We'll be back later."

I considered what she told me about finding the dog. It wasn't unusual for dogs to be stolen and ransomed. I cooperated on that case with Dr. Hannah, after all. Perhaps someone saw a well-behaved dog roaming around Lily's neighborhood and had taken advantage. Friday, or Max, could have jumped out of the car the first chance he got and abandoned his dog nappers.

I decided to call Allie Sands, where I knew Lily would be happy to learn her dog, Max, had been found. Allie was a girlfriend in my past life as a big-city cop. We'd worked together solving murders, she as a coroner and me as a detective. We eventually became involved, but it didn't end well for either of us.

I congratulated Allie her on her engagement to Warren. I teased her about admiring his six-pack abs so long ago while we were vacationing at the resort where Warren ran the store on the wharf.

There was too much time and life between then and now, and here she was about to marry the man after hiring him away from the resort. Warren Jeffrey took over the dive business Allie and her brother Hank started. His experience turned it into a going concern.

Warren and I had been good friends, too. He helped me get through a lot, until finally, fed up with life and love and death, I pulled up stakes and left the resort. I was fed up with being the go-to guy to take care of miscreants, thieves, and other bad boys and girls. I never returned.

Allie talked a blue streak at the prospect of her upcoming wedding. She sounded happy, finally, something I could never do for her.

"Warren left me a voice mail. Do you know what it's about?"

"Not a clue, Jim. Maybe about the wedding?" she asked.

"All right. I'll call him after I talk to Lily about Max."

"That little girl is going to be so happy to know Max hasn't disappeared forever. What's his owner like?"

"Well, she isn't happy, I can tell you that. In fact, she's devastated. Maddie is prepared to give up the dog, though."

"Maddie?"

"Yes. My new partner in the business."

"Is that why you didn't get back to us about coming to the wedding?"

"I don't know, Allie. There are no hard feelings. You know that. Warren and I got along. We still get along. I remembered your comment about his six-pack abs and laughed. I envy him. I'm happy for you."

"So then, you'll be sure to bring Maddie as your plus-one." It wasn't a question.

"I'll be plus-two, sweetheart. I'll be bringing Max, too."

"Lily is going to be crazy with worry until Max shows up. You know that, right?"

"I expect so. I should talk to her and explain."

"All right. I'll get her for you."

I waited, thinking about Maddie and wondering how I would ever make losing Friday up to her. She loved Friday. Or Max, as Lily named him. Maddie loved the dog, whatever his name was. That was clear the first time I saw the two of them together.

"Hi Uncle Jim." Lily was out of breath.

"Hi Lily. How are you?"

"I'm good. I'm missing a dog, though. Max ran away. Or someone took him. I think someone must have stole him. Why would a good dog run away from someone who loves him?"

"Well, maybe he thought the person he ended up with needed him more than you did. There are people like that. Dogs, too. They have a powerful sense of love and affection, you know."

"Maybe." Lily didn't sound convinced.

"In any case, I have a surprise for you. I found Max."

Lily screamed into the phone, loud and piercing and happy. Maddie and Friday chose that moment to walk into the office. The dog slurped up water. Maddie looked at me quizzically.

"I'm going to put you on speaker, Lily. The person who found Max is here with me. Her name is Maddie. And she calls her dog Friday."

Maddie didn't appear happy to be put on the spot. Friday, on the other hand, perked up his ears and plopped down beside the phone. If he could talk, it would be more than the woofs and the whimpering he was doing at the sound of Lily's voice.

"How did you find out he was mine, Uncle Jim?"

"I took him to a veterinarian for a checkup. Don't worry, there's nothing wrong with him. He's fine. Maybe a few extra pounds on both of us that neither of us needs."

"Zelda misses you, Uncle Jim, but we're taking good care of her."

Friday woofed when he heard Zelda's name, too.

"Thank you, Lily. Thank James for me too, okay?"

"I will," she said.

"Friday's ears perk up and he wags his tail every time you talk. He knows it's you."

"Thank you for telling me that, Uncle Jim. I'm glad it was you who found him for me."

"I'm going to put Maddie on now, okay? I need to talk to Allie again when you're finished."

Lily and Maddie gently fenced back and forth. I knew Lily well enough. I could tell by the tone of her voice she was sizing Maddie up. Not surprised, I knew Maddie was doing the same. I stayed out of it.

"I'll make sure to bring your dog and your Uncle Jim home in time for the wedding," Maddie finally admitted to Lily. "I'm going to be his plus one."

Maddie gave me the look as though I'd been keeping something from her. Which I was until she found out about the wedding on her own.

Allie's voice came through loud and clear. Lily must have put the phone on speaker, too. "Good. This is Allie. You're officially invited, Maddie. And Friday or Max, too. See if you can kick the butt of the man standing beside you. All three of you are welcome any time. I'll see that the trailer is cleaned up and ready. You can all stay right here."

Lily's excited *Max is coming home!* was the last thing I heard as Maddie thanked Allie for the invitation. Friday barked and began pacing back and forth around the office until the phone went dead.

"Well, I guess I'm going to have to give up my faithful Friday. Look at him when he recognized Lily's voice." Maddie wasn't in a good mood.

"Don't be so sure. Lily has a life of her own. She's older now. She's probably interested in boys. Or more likely, the boys are interested in her."

I hugged Maddie tight. "When she sees how the two of you are together, I'm sure she'll think hard about leaving you without a dog. Lily is that kind of person."

"If you say so. Now tell me about Warren's six-pack abs, pudgy Mr. Detective."

She dug into my ribs with a finger. I looked at her suspiciously. "Those are ribs. My abs are around the front. And you were eavesdropping."

She grinned. Taking his cue from his mistress, Friday barked. I grinned right back.

"Warren is Allie's department. You should have asked her. Since we're going to the wedding, maybe you'll get a chance to see them for yourself if he takes his shirt off."

"Yeah. No. I like your pudgy abs just fine." She reached to scratch me behind the ear, and I tapped the floor with a foot. That always got her.

"You need a shave."

"I don't have time right now. I have to call Warren."

"That's the guy who left the message. The groom, right?"

"Yeah. He's the one marrying Allie."

"You don't look so good, shamus."

Okay, so maybe I wasn't ecstatic that Allie was marrying my friend. I truly was happy for her. I was feeling a little sorry for myself, too, what with Maddie going to lose Friday, and me losing Allie for good. I sure wasn't about to reveal that to the woman standing in front of me. "I'm okay. Put on something special tonight. We're going to celebrate."

That was all Maddie needed. She left me with Friday and headed down the stairs faster than a speeding bullet. If I knew her, she'd be shopping for most of the afternoon.

I couldn't wait to see what she brought home.

FOUR

I finally played Warren's brief message, thanks to Maddie's insistence. There was nothing to give away the reason for the call. We had been good friends in the past. My expectation was that he wanted to give me a heads up about the upcoming wedding.

To be truthful, the wedding wasn't news to me. Allie hired Warren away from the resort hotel to manage the dive shop she started as part of her successful boat rental and tour business on the panhandle. I knew they had developed a thing. I was happy for both of them. I was a lot happier now that I knew they were making it official.

Allie deserved to be happy. So did Warren. If they found happiness together, who was I to throw cold water on it? Both of them were my friends. Both of them deserved their happiness wherever they found it.

I answered the ringing phone and Warren's familiar deep voice gave me an exuberant greeting. I gave it right back to him. "I was just thinking about you, lucky man."

We went back and forth about stealing my girl and how she deserved better than me. I ended up letting him know how happy I was they finally found each other. It was all true, too, and with that out of the way, I asked about the cryptic voicemail.

"Yeah. About that."

I let him go on.

"A reporter came to see me. She was talking around some old shit. Asking about Pilar and you and the accident and the decision by the authorities to identify the plane crash as the result of a terrorist attack."

"That's old news, Warren."

I didn't go into it with him, but it took me a long time to fix a wrong that included calling the woman I loved and my wife a terrorist. I handled that problem the only way I knew how. Revenge is best served up in the belly of an alligator.

"The reporter was talking to Erica, too, and asking about Kara."

That one was resolved by Pilar and me a long time ago. We flew down and traipsed the length of the Baja to Cabo and then up to Todos Santos. Thanks to the padre at the local mission, we determined that my wedding to Kara and the records the woman left behind for me were a complete fabrication.

"Interesting. That's all old history now. I wonder what she really wanted."

"She asked about Kara's son, James, as well."

Thanks to Allie and DNA testing by one of her connections, she proved that James couldn't be my son. I never learned who his father was. Erica, Kara's sister and James' aunt, took him in unreservedly. He was part of the Sands family now, since Erica had married Hank, Allie's brother.

"I wonder why a reporter is bringing up old wounds? She must have a burr in her pants about something," I told him.

"That's what I thought, too, Jim. Since you're coming here for the wedding, I thought I'd give you a heads-up. You are coming, right? Allie never got a yes or no out of you."

"I talked to her. We're coming."

"We? Who's we? What are you holding out?"

"Someone who heard about your abs from Allie and thinks mine are better."

"So you've lost some weight."

I could see Warren's grin miles away. "Uhh, I wouldn't say that, exactly."

"Then she loves you too much. She's being kind," he said.

"You always did have a way with words. That's why we're friends. Keep the coffee warm and I'll see you on the wharf, just like old times. You better find an umbrella for me. I'm too old to be baking in the sun these days."

I would be returning to a lot of history with Allie and Warren both. While Allie and I were what I'd call ancient history, Warren was another matter. As my good friend, he had been around for the Pilar and Kara debacle when Kara showed up in her sloop with her son in tow.

Warren was there when Pilar, my pregnant wife, was murdered in the charter plane terror attack. Hell, he was there when I walked away, never to return.

Ancient history. Some of it good. A lot of it not so good.

Was I really over it? Judging by what Warren told me about that reporter, I might not be. Maddie was definitely going to be need-to-know for some of it. I couldn't keep it from her any longer.

The question was, how much do I tell her?

FIVE

I couldn't be certain if we were having a fight or only a disagreement. Over a damned trailer. I had ghosts—old wounds, if you must—still haunting me. Allie and her brother Hank, Erica and her daughter Lily, even Warren, were all a part of it. Perhaps it would be good for me to see them all together, living and laughing and being in love and marrying.

On the other hand, Maddie was convinced there was still something between Allie and me. So maybe it was overdue. And just maybe Maddie was right, but I was resisting. Would I never learn?

"It's a nice trailer. Virtually brand-new," I tried to explain. "You'll like it. So will Friday. You'll see. There's grass and everything."

Grass and everything? If that was the best I could do, Maddie would be out the door in minutes. I was beginning to feel like I was bullying her into staying in the trailer on Allie's property.

"Did you sleep with her in that trailer?"

I hesitated too long. Maddie's nostrils flared, and she wasn't having any of it. She wasn't hearing me, either. "You did, didn't you?"

Her breathing became slow and steady. Damn but the

woman was good. I hung my head like the bad person I was. If I talked myself out of this, I deserved a treat. Immediately, I felt even more guilty for thinking it. Strange how Friday had insinuated his way into my life since he arrived with Maddie.

"I was down and out after Pilar was killed in the plane crash. The authorities branded her a terrorist bomber. Deceased, she had no trial to prove otherwise. It was a crock of shit, and I knew it right off, but I couldn't prove it."

Even with the weight of all of that on me, I had to keep it together. Moving in to the trailer on the marina property was how I did it. It was part of the reason I didn't take to drink. The place wasn't a dump. It was brand new.

It took me years of investigation to put Pilar's killer in my sights. When I finally got him there, I made certain the guilty party received the justice he deserved. Call it trial and execution by alligator, but it inflamed the cockles of my heart to have witnessed it firsthand.

I didn't tell Maddie that part of it. She didn't need to know. No one needed to know other than the people who were there to witness the man's demise.

Was the woman going to buy any of it? Time would tell, I guess.

SIX

I hauled in the pile of luggage, all of it new but mine, and realized Maddie had relented. There was no doubt she was coming. She even dug out the bag I picked up for Friday when we went off on our disastrous ski lodge holiday. Like a lost dog, Friday was sitting beside it, looking forlorn.

"No, Friday. We're not going on an airplane."

We hadn't talked about it past the phone call with Allie, but I knew Maddie had been out shopping up a storm. "There won't be any snow for you to plop your big fat bum in, either, dog."

Friday didn't look like he believed me. On the other hand, what woman would venture into the territory of a woman who had been a previous partner to her man without a fresh wardrobe? I knew that much about women. "How long are you planning on staying? Judging by the weight of these bags—"

Maddie gave me the look and I let it go. She was doing a number on me. So was Friday. He never left Maddie's side the entire time. Now I was wondering if Maddie would be staying home in spite of the heavy suitcases she'd allowed me to haul downstairs.

"You bought a new bag." More than one, in fact. They

were hard-sided and looked expensive.

"Of course I did. Do you think I was going to show up at your former girlfriend's place carrying a backpack and looking like an infatuated college girl traveling with her professor?"

I wanted to keep it light. I liked her too much. The age difference wasn't so big. What's ten years among lovers and business partners?

"So that's why you bought the suitcases. You're over your infatuation with me and you're going to run away as soon as Friday and I leave for the wedding."

"Sort of. And no. You're not taking Friday anywhere without me. Furthermore, don't be putting crazy ideas in my head about running away. I'm going to be around to torment you for a while."

"Like you tormented me this morning?"

"Oh yeah. Are you going to be able to keep up?" she grinned.

I wanted to put her over my lap and pretend to spank her. I knew where it would lead. "You're beautiful just the way you are. Warren is going to be jealous."

I left the shopping bags for last. She wouldn't let me look in them. In that moment, she surrendered.

"It's stuff. Just stuff. For you. No looking."

"Why can't I open them now?' I wanted to know.

"No, silly. You can't open them now. It's for us for later."

"I didn't get you anything." Perhaps a little guilt on my part would help.

"I didn't expect you to. Let's go. Friday is champing at the bit. Are we going to put the top down?"

Discretion being the better part of valor, Friday knew enough not to call shotgun. The instant I opened the door, he jumped in the back and settled in, content and anxious as I was to get going. I was sure it was only because he knew we weren't headed for the airport. Or the vet.

Maddie slid across the Packard's seat, looking like a 40s movie star. The top went down, and she settled in beside me, hip glued to hip. I started to feel like a teenager in love all over again. Once out of the city, the old Packard settled in nicely at ten over, running like a top.

Maddie's head rested on my shoulder. Friday woofed his approval from the windy back seat, where he sat with his head over the side. When the first break arrived, we stretched our legs. I picked up road trip munchies while Maddie picked out a couple of music CDs in the truck stop.

"I didn't know you were old-school that way."

"I saw the player in the dash. No sense in letting it go to waste, is there?"

"The new radio has Bluetooth. I'm not so out of the loop as that."

By the time we were out of music, we were at the next stop. We cruised slowly past a couple of local PD cruisers and I pulled up to the pumps. The Packard gobbled fuel like an old farm tractor. I paid and parked the car.

Maddie and Friday got out and headed for the facilities together. I got the idea he was being overly protective, but what did I know? Friday was obviously Maddie's dog—at least, I hoped he would be if I knew Lily.

We didn't bring Friday into the restaurant. With the top down on the Packard, we weren't worried anyone would fault us for mistreating our dog.

SEVEN

Fueled, **fed, walked** and watered, we were ahead of schedule and ready to relax on the last leg of our drive. I pulled out of the truck stop and made for the highway.

The two black and whites we passed when we entered the truck stop pulled out behind us. That there were two of them was no cause for concern. Thus I didn't think anything of it. Everyone had a job to do and breaks to take, and now, like us, their break was over and they were going back to work.

I set my foot on the Packard's pedal for two under and wished them good luck. They didn't try to overtake. They didn't try to pass.

"Did you take it upon yourself to dial 911 after our argument?"

Maddie looked at me and grinned. "It wasn't an argument. It was a discussion. Should I be concerned about being loaded onto a boat, tied with weights and forced to walk the plank once you get me where you want me?"

"I don't know about that. I think putting you over my knee would be a better plan."

"You already did that, remember? You're not going senile on me, are you?"

I checked the mirror. "We have a couple of black and whites behind us. They've been with us since we pulled out of the last stop."

She turned to look back and slid away from me. "Maybe they think you're someone else."

"Me? What about you? You're the one traveling with the stolen dog."

"Very funny. Oh-oh. There goes the blues."

Maddie called it. I had an itch to know how the Packard would perform against modern-day equipment. I resisted the urge to floor it in the huge, overpowered car. A cruiser stayed on our tail. A second pulled up beside us. The siren wailed. I slowed, pulled over and stopped. "There's something going on. Put your hands on the dash and don't move. Do it now."

Maddie called to the dog. "Friday. Sit. Stay."

"Another ten miles and we would have been home free. I wonder what they want."

It was unusual. The police were a long way from home when they picked us up at the truck stop. They obviously knew we were on our way. Now I wanted to know the reason for stopping us.

I didn't get a chance to ask. Two officers approached with sidearms drawn and aimed. "Get out of the car. Now. Do it now."

EIGHT

Maddie and I knew the procedure well. We kept our hands in plain sight and eased out the driver's side, one at a time. We went down on our knees. From the back, Friday kept his eyes on Maddie. He was waiting for a signal.

"You're both under arrest," officer beefsteak announced.

"Why are we being detained? What are the charges?" I asked.

Our questions were met with silence.

"Jimbo. How far away is Lily?"

I pictured Friday's ears perk up in the back of the Packard on hearing the girl's name.

"Eight or ten miles. Why?" I think Maddie knew we were in deep shit before I did. She called to the dog. "Friday."

In the back seat the dog barked and got up on all fours. Every muscle tensed and his ears perked. His tail went straight in the air and stayed there.

"Find Lily. Go. Find Lily."

Friday leaped into action. He flew out of the car. He landed on all fours and didn't stop to be protective of his mistress. He wasn't bothering to wait around. He made for the hills, full speed ahead, hell-bent on doing as his mistress commanded.

Twin taser tags hit Maddie in the back. She collapsed on the ground, twitching and grimacing.

"Don't say a word, sad sack, or you'll end up on the ground with your woman."

Gunshots rang out as one of the police goons fired randomly in Friday's direction. The magazine emptied and he replaced it, but by then it was too late. Friday was long gone. The radio call went out advising whoever was managing the dog and pony show that the clown-car cops had failed to corral the dog part of it.

"Get the woman up."

Immediately it became apparent there were no recordings being made. Maddie moaned and stayed put. The dumb ox cop pulled the trigger and zapped her again when she didn't react to his command. A wet spot spread over the crotch of her pants.

The discussion ended there and we were picked up and flung into the back of the cruiser. In solidarity with my partner, I pissed my pants in protest. In this heat, by the end of tomorrow the four-wheel piss palace would be unbearable.

Maddie slid against me. I told her what I did and she grinned in her own damp solidarity. She let go with whatever remained in her bladder.

"High five, girl. We're on a roll."

"It's gonna have to be a low five in these cuffs. And I don't like your rolls."

"Strange. I recall it was only a few days ago when you were telling me how much you admired my abs."

"I think those were your ribs, dear. They were too hard to be your abs."

"It's a good thing I love you or I'd make a formal request for another car. Speaking of which, isn't it unusual for two perps to be in the back of the same car?

Unless the procedures have changed."

"I have to pee again," she announced.

"Let fly. While you're doing that, do you have any idea why we're here?"

"Nope. Not a one. But I wouldn't be surprised if the gun in my purse was next on the agenda."

"Don't worry about it. You're legal. So am I. It's a part of our job, remember?"

She gave me a look that said I had to be deaf, dumb, and stupid. How could a woman do that to a man with only a single glance every damn time?

"Yeah, I'm thinking that isn't going to work, but you keep right on believing it. How do we get a lawyer to come out to this dog and pony show?"

"We have to be charged. Well, under normal circumstance. I'm not so sure now. Maybe we're being shipped off to the gulag. I hear it's a very popular place these days."

"That's good. We can parent some of those children in concentration-camp cages the government is so proud of."

I shut up and started thinking. Could the mess we were in have anything to do with the heads-up Warren passed along about the reporter? What dark places did she uncover when she started researching me?

"Do you think Friday will be able to find Lily, Jim"

"He'd better or I'll never scratch him behind the ears again. Speaking of which, neither of us will be able to from a jail cell. *Habeas corpus*, anyone?"

The cruisers crossed the divide and headed in the direction of the town we had only recently passed through.

"And here we go. Next stop, perdition."

NINE

From the back seat of the cruiser, it looked to be a sleepy little town. It was off the interstate, where the road through was tagged as the B-route. Dusty streets. A couple of old-time gas stations that the big names in petrol forgot about. Plenty of flags flying to celebrate something or other that was of import to the residents.

Our personal transport vehicle pulled up in front of a newer building. Two stories. Not so many windows to look out on the village. I knew right off the money to build it didn't come from local taxes. It was funded by speeding tickets. Probably with the radar re-tuned to show a couple over to take care of everybody.

It was probably a good job for Chief Joe-Bob and the rest of the mayor's relatives. It would provide a car and uniforms and equipment to help the overweight police chief look good in his wrinkled shirt and the clip-on tie with last week's barbecue smeared all over it.

"I get the feeling we're in hillbilly heaven, Maddie. We need to be careful with these people. They're not used to being questioned by anyone. Non-locals pay the fines and leave."

Maddie turned away from the window to look at

me. "I believe you could be right, shamus. Now how are we going to get our asses out of here?"

I checked the clock hanging over the dilapidated city hall. "Depending on how long it takes Friday to find his former mistress, I'd say three or four hours before help arrives."

"Oh great. And the car is out in the middle of nowhere on the interstate."

"That's a good thing. If Friday can convince anyone to follow him, they should twig on it."

"Thanks for that vote of confidence in my dog. How do you know he won't be happy to get home to Lily and plop down in front of a nice warm fire to relax after all the exercise his chubby bottom is getting?"

She was right. Good old Friday was getting a little pudgy around the middle, sort of like I was. "Lily knows we're coming. Everyone knows we're coming. When Friday, or her Max, arrives all by himself, they'll suspect something is up."

"You better be right, shamus. I don't want to be caught out with all of those new clothes and no wedding procession to attend."

"I'd like to let it be known that there are still some shopping bags I haven't been allowed to look in. My gut tells me it's going to be a while until I do. Are you happy now?"

Maddie giggled uncontrollably, more nerves than anything else. "Not particularly, but let me think about it for three or four hours in a hick-town jail with a country bumpkin sheriff. Are you sure you don't know this place? It seems to me like they all know you."

"Know me? What the hell?"

"Well, we're in the back of some podunk town cop car. We're in handcuffs. And I sure as hell never saw the place before today. I drive right through towns like this. I know better."

"So it's all on me. Thanks. I think." She wasn't cutting me any slack.

Our driver parked and led us into the building. The office space was filled with desks. We were forced to make our way through a tight maze on the way to the solitary cell in a back room. The door slammed shut behind us.

"Looks to me like some of the chief's relatives might have a stake in this game."

"You're mistaken, shamus."

"What do you mean? Take a look for yourself."

"You mean all of them. Every last living one." Maddie let out a disgusted sigh.

"We'll have none of that. We're spending our time together. It's called bonding. What other couple can say the same when they end up in jail?"

Maddie shook her handcuffs at me. "We're already bonded, detective."

I wondered how experienced the outfit was, considering we were sharing the only cell.

TEN

Friday kept to the grass on the side of the highway. The ground was softer there, and he could make better time. He ignored speeding cars and honking horns overtaking him. Eventually, he was able to find his way off the busy four-lane highway and onto a back road.

When he became winded, he halted his quick gallop and slowed to a fast trot, ears forward, tail high in the air like a wind vane as it slowly moved back and forth in rhythm with his body.

He was searching for Lily now. The marina. All the familiar scents and smells and odors that went with it. He recognized the diner smells on the road to the marina and picked up speed. By the time he found himself in the marina compound, he was panting and exhausted.

He barked. It was his way of announcing he was home to anyone paying attention.

Once. Twice. Three times.

Zelda followed Zoe as both dogs scampered out to greet Max's familiar bark. They rubbed noses and nudged and barked and generally made a fuss. Lily came out to see what the commotion was about and recognized her dog.

"Max! You're home."

Lily dropped to her knees and the dog ran to her. Her

arms circled the wayward dog. He licked at her face and sat down to catch his breath. Lily looked around the parking lot, expecting to see a fancy convertible. Confused, she queried the dog. "Where's Uncle Jim? Where's Maddie?"

Max bumped noses with Zelda and Zoe. He led the dogs on a chase to Allie's car in the lot and back to Lily.

"Max. You're panting too hard. You need water. You're dehydrated. How far did you run? Come on. You have to rest. Your dish is waiting."

Max ran to greet Allie. Still panting, still with his tongue hanging out. His teeth closed on her pant leg. He tugged in an attempt to drag her to the car.

"Lily? What's wrong? Where's Jim and Maddie?"

"They're not here. I think Max ran the whole way by himself."

"Well that's not right. All three of those dogs are upset. Max needs water right now."

A very pregnant Allie hurried off as best she could to find Warren. Lily busied herself watering Max. He drank and went back to running from Lily to the car and back. Allie returned and the dog looked expectantly at her. He sat and barked.

"I think he's trying to tell us something. Come on you guys. We'll all go. Where's Erica? She needs to come with you, Lily."

The women piled into the car. Warren drove. Three dogs hung their heads out the window. Max barked his assent as Warren took them over the back roads to the freeway. He turned in the direction he knew Jim would be taking to get to the marina.

They passed the car pulled off on the opposite side of the highway. Max barked. Warren steered onto the median and burned a quick U-turn. He pulled in behind the Packard in time to meet a flatbed tow truck halting in front of it.

Everyone stay here and hold the dogs. I'll take a quick look-see."

Allie waddled to the car and pulled a handkerchief out of a pocket. She used it to open the dash. It was Jim's car all right, missing his signature handgun. Relieved, she struggled to lean in and remove the keys from the ignition. She walked back to the trunk and opened it. It was filled with luggage. She replaced the keys and approached the tow truck driver.

"What's going to happen to the car?"

"I was told it's being impounded. I'm hauling it to the police lot down the highway a bit."

Allie made for the car. "He's taking it to an impound lot. I expect Jim and Maddie are in a cell somewhere in the next town. They shouldn't be hard to find."

Warren steered around the Packard and reversed course across the median. He made good time to Harpertown.

ELEVEN

Jim and Maddie cooled their heels in the small cell. Requests for phone calls and lawyers were denied or ignored. By hour three, they were still in the dark as to why they had been shanghaied by cops and transported to the local jail. Without warning, a cop marched a woman down the hall and put her in their cell.

"Boy, are you two ever in the shit," she told us. "You should be getting out of this place in five or ten. And I don't mean days."

By all appearances, Maddie didn't take too kindly to someone not involved with their arrest showing they had knowledge of the case. "Are you a cop?"

Th woman said nothing.

"Is that a no? In my world, no response is a response," Maddie explained, before hauling back a fist. She got off a roundhouse punch and decked the woman. Her head banged against the wall and she dropped like a stone.

Officers rushed into the room, unlocked the door to the holding cell, and hauled the woman out. "You're going to jail for a long time. That was a cop you just assaulted."

"Then why did she say she wasn't? Was she lying to us? I have a witness. We want a lawyer right now. Two lawyers. We want to make our phone calls. We want to see a judge. Stop screwing around, you useless bags of crap. And while you're at it, go clean out your cruiser. I pissed all over the back seat."

I waved a hand in the air. "For the record, I second that emotion. What she said. I pissed in your cruiser, too. Call it spite if you must. You have something to do when your shift ends with this podunk outfit."

"Careful, dearest. You're insulting all the towns called Podunk."

I banged a leftover tin cup left behind by a previous occupant across the bars. I'd seen it done in old movies by protesting inmates. No one paid any attention. Not even Maddie.

So here I was. In jail. With Maddie. Friday gone AWOL. It was looking like we weren't going to make the wedding I promised to attend. I wondered who Allie would get to give her away.

And then there was Warren. I was supposed to be his best man, and here we were in jail like we partied our hearts out on stag night.

I was wondering if this might be some kind of wedding prank.

TWELVE

Lily's skinny legs scurried out of the car ahead of everyone. Three fur-covered bodies rushed after the girl, not wanting to be left behind for the adventure they suspected was coming. Lily held the door for her motley collection and the foursome rushed the police station's front desk.

Erica called to her daughter. "Lily. Don't be so quick to go in there by yourself, dear."

Allie admonished her friend. "That girl. She's just like her mother. And I'm looking at you, Erica."

The women laughed and followed the girl and the trio of sniffing and snuffling dogs into what passed for reception. A sole officer occupied a desk in a far corner of the room. He took in the dogs and the girl and the two women. The expression on his face said there was trouble coming and he didn't want to be there.

"What's going on? Who are you people? Get those dogs out of here."

Realizing he was outnumbered, the officer's hand moved to the taser on his belt. Lily's stern voice commanded the dogs to halt and sit. Silenced by the girl's command, they obeyed. A look of relief took over the nervous officer's face, and he was about to sit down, too.

He realized his mistake and straightened.

Tears streamed down Lily's face, and she began to sob. Three pairs of dog ears perked up, but they remained sitting at attention. "Where's Uncle Jim. Where's my Uncle Jim? What have you done to him? Where is he?"

Allie and Erica stepped in front of the girl. "I'm Allie Sands. This is Lily's mother, Erica. The dogs belong to us. A friend is waiting out front in the car. We want to see the couple in your jail cell."

Allie's rapid-fire questions didn't appear to affect the pudgy officer in his sweat-stained shirt. He held up a hand, but he was too late to interrupt.

"I've called a lawyer. She's on her way. So far, the count appears to be this: Three women, three dogs, and a single police officer. Does that sound about right? Furthermore, who's in charge of this dog and pony show? Is your top pony around, or is he hiding out in a barn somewhere? He obviously can't be good enough for a doghouse.

As though to back her up, the dogs barked in unison. Lily called to silence them. "Good dogs. Stay."

The dogs obeyed. The deputy relaxed only a little. "Well ma'am—"

It was Erica's turn to take the brown-shirted ball of sweat to task. "Do we look like ma'ams to you, officer? The woman asked you a question. Answer it. And I have a question of my own. Where's Jim Nash being held? Is he in your jail or not? And keep in mind we have a lawyer coming."

The cop flushed a bright pink and moved to pick up the desk phone, then thought better of it. "If you all will just be patient and follow me, I'll take you to him."

Three women quick-stepped through the maze of desks and chairs. Three dogs with tails straight up in the air trotted after the women. Alerted by the commotion, Jim and Maddie made to stand to greet the arriving delegation.

A grinning Jim rattled his tin cup against the bars. He began singing an off-tune version of an old song. *"Nobody knows the trouble I've seen—"*

Through the bars, Maddie recognized a very pregnant woman and safely assumed that was the bride to be.

"The things you put a woman through on her wedding. Jim Nash, you should be ashamed."

He hung his head and cocked an eyebrow, pretending guilt and feigning innocence. Allie reached through the bars and the women introduced themselves.

Lily couldn't believe Jim was in a jail. "Uncle Jim, what did you do this time? Why is Maddie in prison with you? Are you going to be eating gruel again?"

A grinning Maddie added to his embarrassment. "Yes, Uncle Jim. Do explain to us what you did to put us in prison. Please admit your guilt so we all can get out of here for the wedding."

"It's not prison, Lily. It's only jail," Jim explained.

Lily appeared doubtful. "It looks like prison to me, Uncle Jim. It has bars."

Erica chimed it with some chiding of her own. "She's right. It's a prison as far as we're concerned. Allie already called Kasidi. She's on her way."

Erica stuck her hand past the bars and introduced herself to Maddie. "I'm so sorry this had to happen to you. What's going on? What did Jim do?"

Maddie looked at Erica and shrugged. "Nothing as far as we know. I haven't done anything either, other than get tasered like a schoolgirl for talking."

She raised her voice for all to hear. "For crying out loud, where do these hillbillies come from?"

'Kasidi should be here any minute. If Jim is smart, he'll let her handle it. Just don't let him argue about her bill."

Allie felt an explanation was in order. "There's a reason we have a lawyer on call for Jim." She grinned at

Maddie. "Kasidi got Lily's Uncle Jim out of a pickle a few years ago. She's a good lawyer and a friend of mine to boot. I'm sorry to meet you and run, Maddie, but I've got three angry dogs and three angry people. If we aren't careful, we'll all be in a cell with you and I have a business to run. And, oh yeah, a wedding to attend to."

Maddie gave Jim the evil eye before breaking into a wide smile. "Where's Warren, Allie?"

"He's out in the car. He thought it best to lie low in case he had to bail all of us out."

"A wise man indeed if I know all of you," Jim said. "Pass along my regards and let him know I hope to see him on the wharf soon."

Allie passed a phone through the bars. "Make any calls you have to before they find it. Kasidi's number is in there somewhere, too. The trailer is ready whenever you do your prison break. I wish I could do more."

Lily wasn't sure what to make of Allie's prison break comment. "See? I said you were in prison. You're going to have to do a prison breakout. But it's okay, Uncle Jim. I don't think you're a bad person. You either, Maddie. Max is fine. He's waiting for you in the lobby. He ran all the way to find us and then he led us back to you and to Maddie. Warren drove all of us. I wanted to bring Friday to see you, but my mom thought he should stay there." Lily was breathless when she finished.

"Thank you, Lily. I'm sure Uncle Jim is grateful, too. Friday is a good dog, isn't he?"

Lily wasn't sure what to say when Maddie called her dog Friday, so she didn't say anything.

Jim began singing a refrain that was only a little familiar. It was something about trouble and nobody seeing it. Allie shook her head. "Maybe you could bring Maddie a change of clothes. I need one too. We urinated all over the back of the car that transported us."

"I'll try to get your bags. No promises. You're likely to

be in jumpsuits by then. If I manage, I'll send Warren back. He's a lot more patient, unlike you. And me."

She looked at Jim, but her words were for Maddie. "Try not to let him fly off the handle."

"Yeah, I know. I've been working on him with limited success."

"All right, you two. I'm right beside you. Is Friday all right?"

"Max is good. We brought all three dogs with us. Zelda and Zoe and Max are out front causing a stink. If these Keystone cops don't know trouble when they see it, they're dumber than a bag of hammers."

Allie took two steps before turning back. "Call Kasidi now. Right now. Maddie, make him do it."

"Well, the man sure doesn't have anything else to do. Jim? It's on you," Maddie insisted.

Allie turned back a second time. "The wedding isn't going to happen until both of you are present and accounted for, understood?"

"Does that mean if we get twenty-five to life, you'll be an old maid?" Jim wisecracked.

"Not on your life, Nash. Do your duty with Kasidi and get both your butts out of jail. Don't let it be like last time and take it upon yourself to do everything."

The women high fived through the bars and pregnant Allie waddled down the hall to the door.

"She's one tough cookie. And extremely pregnant. What did you do to let her get away, detective?"

I might not know much, but I knew enough to change the subject. "I have to call my lawyer."

THIRTEEN

I made the smart choice and called Kasidi Beale. She was on her way, but she wasn't about making promises to get us released until she knew more. I didn't make the joke about not paying if she was wasting my time, and she reassured me she would be here shortly.

With nothing on an empty plate in a jail cell with a population of two, I brought up Warren's phone call with Maddie.

"I thought it was about wanting you as best man," she said. She was convinced.

"Well, that was part of it. The other part was about a reporter sniffing around, asking too many questions about my past."

"Such as?"

Maddie knew about Kara. I spared her most of the details about Pilar. And I never mentioned anything concerning the demise of Nicolas senior. In my estimation, that would be a bad idea, no matter what.

Still, my bets were on the reporter. Going by what Warren said, she could be on to Nicolas' death in the swamp. But how? Who did she know? What did she know?

Warren had been concerned enough to call and warn

me. But even he couldn't know the worst of it. Perhaps he was going on the behavior he witnessed at the resort when I got news of Pilar's death. If that was the case, he was right to be concerned.

"If these guys toss the car, they'll find our handguns. Your paper is in order, right? You got the renewal from Boyle? He brought it over in person."

"Yes, dear. Everything is in order," she assured Jim. Maddie smiled sweetly and broke into a grin. She couldn't help it. "I so enjoy saying that to you. You have no idea."

I smiled back, but I was deep in thought. It had to be about Nicolas. A relative, perhaps. Or a town full of enough of his relatives to populate the police department. Maybe the reporter was related, too.

"I think we're in trouble, Maddie."

Now I had to figure out how much to tell her. But first I needed confirmation that this dump was full of Nick senior's relatives. I recognized a voice calling my name and put it on the back burner. "Well if it isn't my shyster lawyer. It's about time you showed. Did you bring any fireworks this time?"

Maddie was quick to jump on me. "That's no way to talk about your lawyer. At least, not while she's in the same room."

"Now there's a woman you should listen to, Nash. Hi. I'm Kasidi Beale, and I'm the shyster here to help you." Maddie and Kasidi grinned back and forth and introduced themselves before reaching through the bars to shake hands. It seemed to me they'd already come to an understanding.

"What did Nash do that you ended up in jail, Maddie?"

"I'm not sure and you should know everyone is asking that same question. Judging by what he said, do I need a different lawyer?" Maddie grinned at Kasidi.

"Not unless you want to stay a few extra days. I have

writs of *habeas,* Jim. You two should be out shortly. Did the local yokels happen to mention any charges? High crimes and misdemeanors? Arson? Kidnapping? Failing to pay your lawyer?"

"Get us out of here, lawyer. We need to pause and regroup. And that's the most begging you're going to hear me do."

"I'm thinking Maddie is going to be trouble. I heard she decked a female cop. Good going. I'd have done the same thing."

It was my turn to grin. Maddie had to know she was as important in my life as ever. I'm not out of here until Maddie is out. You're right about the trouble part, though. She's been nothing but since I hired her."

Kasidi grinned so hard her face had to be hurting. "Yeah, no. That trouble bit you mentioned is hard to believe. I was here for your last visit, remember? A house burned down with you in it. While that was going on, a trucker with a mobile slaughterhouse had Allie strapped onto a stainless steel operating table. Does that jog your memory at all?"

I waved an admonishing finger at Kasidi. "Maddie doesn't need to know all our secrets until I can spin them my way. And I need a meeting with you, stat."

"Well, I'll be at the wedding if you can wait."

I thought for a minute. "Yeah, no. It could be more urgent than that."

I didn't say more. I didn't want to alarm Maddie, even if she was regarding me with a wide-eyed look of shock.

Or maybe it was horror.

FOURTEEN

Lawyer Kasidi Beale was as good as her word. Maddie and I eavesdropped from our jail cell. It took a lot of talking, a bunch of listening, and a fair amount of bluster, but she talked her way to getting us released. Sadly, it didn't happen before we were assigned jail-house jumpsuits. Our perp walk to freedom saw us stripping naked before making our way past the jumble of desks in the overcrowded front office.

"For sure this place is full of nepotism. Why else would there be so many desks in such a tiny office?"

Kasidi knew me well enough to wait at the door to the station. She greeted us before we could make our way outside. "Are you two nuts? Don't move a muscle until I get some blankets. They'll have you back for public indecency in a New York minute. Did you collect your personal effects?"

A Keystone cop blushing bright pink handed over two bags and by then Kasidi was back with the blankets.

"Do you keep these on reserve in your car?"

Kasidi grinned at Maddie. "I've had dealings with Jim before. I'm quite familiar with his methods."

"More like antics from what I've seen," Allie said. "We need to have coffee some time. We can trade war stories."

"I'm standing right here, you two," Jim said sheepishly.

"Maddie, we can get together with Allie at the reception. That should put the fear of the lord into both Jim and Warren."

The women high fived, and I was left carrying the property bags as Kasidi escorted us to our car.

Kasidi gave Jim's old Packard an appraising look. "Nice ride, Nash. You must be in the money. Speaking of which, my normal fee—"

"Not so fast, Kasidi. You have a normal fee? If I remember right, your normal fee is whatever you feel like charging."

"Exactly, Jim. Whatever the traffic will bear. And seeing what you drive in traffic—"

Maddie laughed.

"Now get dressed and get going. You two have a wedding to attend," Kasidi reminded the pair.

Our arrival at the marina was anti-climactic. Our attendance at Allie's wedding had been telegraphed. Lily had briefed James on her prison escapade. Friday enthusiastically rushed out to greet Maddie. He only touched a cold nose to my hand before wandering off to make fresh acquaintances with the rest of the litter he left behind when he deserted.

Maddie wasted no time examining the trailer from the outside. She walked from one end to the other. Looked over the grounds. Swung a foot at the tree hard enough to shake the leaves. Looked at me.

I recognized the look. It said hotel.

"You expect me to stay in that? I'm not staying in a trailer where you spent time with you-know-who, shamus. Get a grip."

"It's a beautiful trailer. Look at it. There's a nice green lawn. A leafy tree for shade. There are plenty of flowers in the yard. Wait until you see the inside," I tried explaining.

"I'm not setting foot in it, and that's that." Maddie's hands went to her hips and she crooked a knee.

It meant defeat—for me, not her. I hauled out my phone and searched for a hotel. I was on hold to make a reservation for two when Allie appeared out of nowhere, looking very big and very pregnant.

"You never told me you were here, Jim."

Like it was my fault.

"Come on, Maddie. I'll take you on a tour."

I swear it couldn't have been more than five minutes before the women returned. Maddie looked at me quizzically.

"Who are you calling?" she wanted to know.

"A hotel. I thought—"

"You can stay in a hotel if you want to. I'll be staying here."

I was saved when Lily showed up with three familiar dogs. Zoe and Zelda licked my hand, but it was Zelda who stayed by me. I scratched at the back of her head and she nuzzled my thigh. The old girl seemed as pleased to see me as I was to see her. "It sounds like you're in the dog house again, Uncle Jim."

In that case, maybe Zelda would let me stay with her.

"Lily, I'm always in trouble with those two. I've learned to live with it. Help me carry the bags into the trailer, please, before Maddie changes her mind. Again." I tossed the woman side-eye, and was ignored for my effort.

Zelda sat down beneath the tree.

Maddie's side-eye followed me into the trailer. I called back to Lily. "The one good thing is that the dog house is full of dogs. There's no room for me, Lily."

Lily wisely didn't say a word. Maddie had no shortage. "Don't count on it, sailor. The week isn't over yet."

I took the rest of the bags out of the car and Lily help haul the lighter ones into the trailer. I had to pass the tree. It wasn't huge, but in time it would be. "Lily? Who planted the tree?"

"Yeah, we caught Zelda up here more than a few times. She'd come up and sit and look over the dock and the water like she was waiting for the sun to set. It was my idea to give her shade. Now Zelda and Zoe both come up here and lay down under it sometimes.

"I think it's a grand idea. Zelda is getting old. I'm going to plant a chair under that thing and grow old, too. Want to join me?"

"I would, Uncle Jim, but I have chores. Maybe later if you're still allowed near the trailer." The miniature devil-girl giggled and ran off. Three happy dogs trotted after her.

"What's for dinner, cutie-pie?" My second devil-girl had spoken.

"How about Chinese? Would you mind if I call down to the rest of the bums in this dive and find out if they'd like to join us? Maybe we can bring out the table and chairs and set up beneath that nice green tree."

The entire crowd showed. People and kids and dogs talked and laughed and woofed and snorted while kids chased around, followed by the dogs. I was proud to know them all, and I think Maddie was, too. She and Allie and Erica sat off to the side and traded war stories about their men. The men tried their best to ignore the stories.

Eventually, the dogs hogged the shade beneath the tree. No one minded. Warren and Hank and I sat in the shade under an umbrella and traded lies about past lives. The kids floated back and forth between tables, talking and laughing and just being kids.

It was good to see every one of them, and I was glad I showed for the wedding. From what I could tell, Maddie was, too.

FIFTEEN

I woke in a panic, struggling to breathe. Maddie was stretched across my body. A bony elbow dug into my stomach. Her full weight leaned on me. It brought her level with the window sill. A fog of breath coated the window as she looked out into the dark yard. "What are you doing, woman? There's a bathroom in here. You don't have to go outside." I gasped for breath, and she eased herself off me.

"Jim. I swear. Take a look for yourself. There's a car outside."

"Where's the hardware?" I slipped my robe over my shoulders and made for the door.

"We're at a wedding, remember? I left it in the trunk where it belongs," she said.

"The lights should be on." The yard lights were fixed with motion detectors.

"The lights?"

"Yeah. With all the valuable boat properties on the property, Allie had lights installed years ago. They come on if someone comes onto the property at night."

"Well, shamus, there's no light now."

"Very good, detective. It's a gold star for you. Fortunately, we have a full moon."

I made for the door.

"You better belt that robe before you go out, sailor. The full moon is going to be shining down on your naked bits."

I opened the door and listened. A car started. My gaze shifted toward the parking lot. Headlights backed out of the driveway and disappeared. It could have been a wrong turn. Still, with everything going on—

"We definitely had visitors. I'm going to find Warren."

Maddie sat up in bed. "You're going to find Warren? I think we both know where he is. You can find him in the morning at the breakfast table. We've been invited."

Sidetracked, I knew to change the subject. "That's nice. I meant to ask you. What did you and Allie talk about? You sure changed your mind in a hurry about staying in a hotel."

"I did no such thing. It's all your imagination."

"Yes dear. Good night." I knew when to surrender, too.

SIXTEEN

I was enjoying a nice leisurely breakfast on the wharf with old friends when Maddie led me away from the breakfast crowd. "What is it now, woman?" I sensed she was still a little uneasy about being the new girl on the block—or, in this case, the marina.

She rolled her eyes at my manly man imitation. "It's Lily. She's been following me around when I'm with Friday. I think she's stalking me. She's definitely spying on me."

"Oh come on. Why would she be stalking you? It's probably because you're new to her and hanging around her place."

"I don't know," she said. "I think I'm going to talk to her mother about it.

"Relax, Mads. She already has Zelda and Zoe to look after. She's probably trying to figure out if you'll be a good fit for her Max. You know how she loves those dogs."

"Yes, I've been watching her with them. They follow her everywhere. Even Friday follows her."

"Now who's the stalker?" I smiled at her.

"Well, I love Friday. I want to be sure he's got a good home when I leave."

"And what do you think so far?" I wanted to know.

"He'll have as good a home here as he always did."

Lily followed after her Max as he sought out a snuffling Maddie. He returned the snuffle and licked her hand. "What's wrong, Auntie Maddie? You look sad."

I was certain Maddie's waterworks were about to start any minute. Lily took her hand and dragged her away. Max followed on the heels of both. They didn't halt so far away that I couldn't hear the two of them. "I've been watching you with Max, Auntie Maddie."

"You have, have you?" Maddie looked at me and smiled.

"Oh yes. I can tell he really likes you. And you like him just as much, I think."

"Well, I miss having him around now that he's home. I only have your Uncle Jim to keep me company. I was so used to having your Max in my life."

"Maybe Max could stay with you in the trailer," Lily said. "Do you think Uncle Jim will go back to prison?"

I was about to interrupt when Maddie held up a hand.

"I think having Max in the trailer would be just grand, Lily, but your Max has been away for a long time. I think he needs to run around with everyone. What do you think?"

"Did you know Zelda is his mother?" Lily asked.

"I didn't know that. Zelda is a pretty grand old dog too, isn't she?"

"Uncle Jim found her and let me take care of her when he went away. James helps, too. We both do."

"You're going to have to tell me all about your Uncle Jim sometime. And all of your dogs, too."

"I don't think I have time right now. It's a pretty long story how Zelda found me in Florida and rescued my mom and we got shot at and then we came here with Aunt Allie and Hank when he married my mom—" Lily went on.

"My goodness. That sounds like quite an adventure."

Maddie looked across at me with a strange look.

I started to worry Lily was talking too much. "So, kids, how's it going?" Yeah, no, that wouldn't work, either. "How's my old girl Zelda? Is James keeping her out of trouble? And Zoe. Is he taking care of her all right?"

Maddie looked from me to Lily and caught her nodding assent. "Who's James? You two sure do have a lot of people in your lives."

"Lily, why don't you let me talk with Maddie for a bit? Now that you let the dog out of the bag, I'm going to have a lot of explaining to do."

"All right, Uncle Jim. Max. You stay. Stay with Maddie. And Uncle Jim, there are no dogs in bags here. We'll talk later, okay, Maddie?"

It was hard to tell who was more enthusiastic, Maddie, or Lily's Max and Maddie's Friday. Lily noticed, too. I hoped she wouldn't be hurt knowing that her Max was still crushing on Maddie.

We spent a long time sitting in front of the trailer. I talked. And talked. And talked. Maddie listened. I don't know who was more exhausted when I finished, but I got it off my chest. Well, most of it, anyway. All the parts I wanted to.

I left out the part about Nick senior and the alligator and a bunch of minor details. I was feeling rather accomplished about it all, too.

A huge yacht eased up to the wharf and Warren jumped off and tied up.

"Is that more guests arriving?" Maddie asked.

"No. That's Warren. With the abs, remember? He was out on a charter with Hank."

Maddie straightened in her chair. "Right. Hank is Erica's husband and Lily's adoptive dad."

"And Allie's brother. You're learning. It's a complicated life I've had until I met you."

"Oh come on. I bet you say that to all the girls.

Breakfast was so busy I only had time to listen. I didn't want to sound nosy among all these new people in my life."

"Well, now that you mention it— "

She poked me in the ribs and I grunted. "I'm going to check out Warren's abs. I need to know if they're the real deal," she said.

"Good. I'll make introductions."

SEVENTEEN

I found it strange that a black SUV drove into the parking lot the instant the yacht docked. Two men wearing suits exited and walked through the crowd gathered for the celebratory breakfast. They halted some distance from where Warren and Hank were tying off the yacht, waiting for passengers to disembark.

Warren didn't appear happy on seeing the waiting men. Neither did Hank. And they became even less so as the suits approached and began talking. I deserted my impromptu stakeout and made my way to the SUV in the parking lot. I snapped a closeup of the plate and checked the grill for lights. I tried four doors. All locked. Satisfied, I returned to the spot where I could keep an eye on the proceedings at the end of the huge wooden wharf.

Things weren't going well. Yelling and shoving and what sounded like threats drifted past the crowd of well-wishers eating their breakfast on the brightly decorated dock. I witnessed Allie turn a concerned eye toward the action. I hurried to the table where she was sitting with Maddie and Erica.

"I'll go see what this is about, Allie. You stay here. You're in no condition to get into a fistfight if it comes to that," I told her.

"You're telling me I'm ten months pregnant, aren't you?"

I thought she was going to cry. "Well, you said it, not me."

"I just want to make it through the wedding, Jim. What happens after that—" She halted.

"I'll see what I can do," I assured her.

I slipped hands into pockets and ambled off toward the action. I tried to appear nonchalant about the whole affair, even with the voices getting louder. I stepped between the two factions. "All right, you two. Enough is enough. There are guests present and your yelling and threats are causing alarm. Take a breath and step back or I'll call the cops."

The men didn't appear happy when I took out my phone and snapped a photo. They directed hard looks at Warren and Hank before hurrying past the breakfast crowd and driving off in the SUV.

"Those two are feds."

"How do you know that?" Hank asked.

"That black SUV in the lot. And the lights under the grill. I checked before I wandered down. You two ought to know that Allie and Erica were paying attention. You were even making Maddie upset. I don't like the women in my life to be upset so close to a wedding. What's going on that you haven't told Allie?"

Warren and Hank exchanged worried glances. I took that to mean the shit was going to be hitting the fan. If it hadn't already.

EIGHTEEN

I was convinced the SUV was Federal. To be certain, I sent the plate off to Boyle, hoping to know if it was in the system. I didn't mention it to anyone. I wanted to be sure before I stuck my uninvited nose in any deeper. I figured the guys could handle it.

Allie, on the other hand, had a wedding to handle. Judging by the size of the woman, she'd be lucky to make wedding day before giving birth. She didn't need crap from anyone on her happy day.

"Just the woman I want to see." I sidled up to Maddie.

"Yes, shamus? You must want something. You're purring like a cat."

"Warren and Hank were arguing with those two men. Were you able to hear anything?"

Maddie was the one sitting closest to the action. Still, she was surrounded by the breakfast chatter too.

"I saw. I couldn't hear much. Allie's table was engrossed in talk about babies and diapers and teething and all kinds of stuff I never want to be forced to hear again. What's going on?"

"I don't know. I spotted a government SUV in the parking lot. The two occupants had words with the guys before I took it upon myself to intervene. I asked them to leave."

"I saw the gesturing and poking. What do you think is going on? Should we be concerned?" she asked.

"I don't want to jump to conclusions. It's a wedding, after all. I don't want to cause problems before Allie gets hitched. If she doesn't give birth first. That woman is as big as a house—not that there's anything wrong with that," I added quickly.

"Yeah, there was talk of that, too. I think I know all the signs, the most important being something about water breaking. What the hell is that about? I don't want to look it up."

"Don't look at me. A book by someone called Dr. Spock will inform you."

"Thanks, but no thanks. Not in my lifetime if I have any say in it. Have you seen Lily?" She changed the subject.

"Are you still spying on Lily and Friday?" I admonished her.

Maddie blushed a bright pink. "Not any more than the stalking she's doing when her Max is hanging with me. My suspicion is that James is in on it, too. Why?"

"The three of you are all peas in the same pod. Did you ever stop to think that the two of them might be spying on you to learn what kind of dog napper you are?"

Immediately she went on the defensive. "Dog napper? I'm no dog napper. Friday jumped into my car. I didn't steal him in a drive-away." She halted, indignant that I brought it up.

"No, no. I mean she might want to see how you treat her Max if you take him away. You know, like you want to know how she'll treat your Friday when you leave him with her."

She shrugged and looked defeated.

"You're three stalkers in my book." It would be

laughable if all three of them weren't serious.

"Yeah, no, if you want to be in my book in that fancy-dancy trailer, a little support for your partner would be appreciated."

"Come on, Maddie. You can't steal a dog, no matter how much you love him. We're both going to wait Lily out and learn what she decides. You know that's the only way to go." She knew I was right. "Why don't you tell her about how you two discovered each other at that rest stop? She'd probably like to hear all about that."

I was this far from telling Maddie what I suspected with the feds running around the property. I didn't want to alarm her. And I sure didn't want her to mention anything to Allie or Erica. The three women were fast becoming friends. Even I knew women who are friends share everything.

I went back to worrying about what Warren and Hank were into, and what the feds were doing wandering around the property. As an afterthought, I asked Maddie not to mention anything to Allie and Erica. By then I wasn't sure she was paying attention.

It seemed to me as though she was rushing off to spy on Lily and Friday.

NINETEEN

All right, so I was putting off everything to the detriment of everyone, including me, because I didn't want to mess up the wedding. Allie would kill me, not to mention what Maddie would do to me now that the women had bonded. Even Lily was on their side, which meant Zelda, Zoe and Friday wouldn't be far behind. Would the dog house be big enough for four?

Warren and Hank were tight. Even though I was good friends with Warren in another life, he wasn't about allowing an interloper like me to interfere in their business now that he was marrying Allie. I couldn't blame him. I wouldn't, either.

Still, there were feds roaming around. Something had to be up. Boyle hadn't got back to me about the license plate. I thought better about sending him a reminder. The man had a real job to do, unlike my best-man duties at a wedding in a far-removed part of the state.

So I sat on the lawn in the shade in front of the big fancy trailer and waited for the dogs to show up. I could always rely on Zelda to come by, wagging her tail and snuffling at my ankles or my fingers as I handed out treats like I was a doggie Santa in the off season.

The old girl was a bear for affection and it tickled me that she remembered me after all these years. Even Zoe was no stinker. She liked to come around, too, but I figured that was only for the treats she knew I kept.

Zelda and Zoe would settle at my feet and it wasn't long before Lily's Max sidled up looking all guilty about having deserted me. Before long he was nosing my hand, looking for a handout, too, as he settled in with the other two. I was in dog heaven. All I had to do was keep the treats coming. I liked to get out of the chair and join them on the ground.

Lily kept finding excuses to visit, too. I'm pretty sure she was checking me out for any signs that her Max didn't want anything to do with me. I think she was disappointed not to find Maddie with us. I knew how hard it would be for her to turn Max over to another person—or if she would even consider it.

It was cute watching her keep an eye on Maddie and Max, too. I sat back and smiled and sometimes grinned and tried not to let her think I was watching her antics. Ditto for Maddie, but I couldn't hide a thing from that one.

All that was the simple part. I still had no clue what it was with the feds wandering around the property. Warren and Hank were no help. They played their cards too close to their chests as far as that went. It was obvious they didn't want my involvement in whatever it was they were into. I was best man and that was it.

Well, I was best man, and I was giving the bride away. There was probably something Freudian in that.

Feeling marginalized, I picked up a couple of tennis balls and proceeded to tease the dogs into a game of fetch. I didn't go too hard. I didn't want to worry faithful, chubby old Zelda into a heart attack. That's when I realized Friday came by his weight problem naturally. When the old girl started panting, I quit and retrieved water for all and we retired to the shade to contemplate a dog's life.

I put my back to the tree, and it wasn't long before my chin dropped to my chest. I was off dreaming about old dogs and new women and former best friends.

TWENTY

I should have stayed in touch with Warren. I did good by him in a past life as a best friend while I lived the Kara and Pilar debacles at the resort hotel. I would have stayed in contact, too, but for one thing. His relationship with Allie. It came as a complete surprise when she told me. In another life Allie and I had been lovers, until I had screwed it up.

That was why I kept away when she made the announcement. I didn't want to chance messing up her life a second time. I couldn't just pop by from time to time to see how both were doing. It didn't feel right.

So here I was, sitting in the shade, growing old with the dogs, and deep in a mid-day snooze. Life was good. Until it wasn't.

"Jim?"

I opened an eye and squinted out at the world. The sun was still out. The sky was still blue. An offshore breeze was fluttering the canvas sun shade. "Yes, Maddie? I'm alive. I was just resting my tired eyes for a minute."

"Uh-huh. You can fool the dogs, but you can't fool me. You're just as tired and sleepy as they are."

I looked down to discover the dogs still at my feet.

"Let sleeping dogs lie, I always said."

Maddie snickered. "I don't think you're going to be able to do that much longer."

"Why do you say that?" I quickly ran through a list in my head. Suit? Check. Shoes? Check. Tie? Check. Rings? Well, they were safe in the trailer. There was no reason to expect them to disappear. To be sure, I turned to look at the trailer. It was still there.

"Allie asked if I knew anything about what was happening on the wharf," Maddie said.

"What did you tell her?" I needed to know if she did as I asked.

"I didn't tell her anything beyond letting her know I witnessed the same thing she did. To be honest, I don't think she believed me. She's looking for you."

I needed to be somewhere else. I had nothing to tell her. Boyle hadn't got back to me. "I'm going to cruise the motels in town. Want to come along?"

"Can we take Lily?"

"Of course. On one condition. Lily doesn't need to know about what happened on the dock."

"Got it. Let's take the dogs, too. I'm sure they'd like a ride in a vintage convertible." I gave Maddie the eye and she flushed and broke into a grin. "Yeah, so my methods might be obvious, but my heart is definitely in the right place. Wouldn't you say, Jimbo?"

How could I say no? "I'll put the top down. Bring water for the dogs when you collect Lily. It'll make points." It was my turn to blush.

"You care for Friday about as much as I do, you old softy."

She jabbed me hard in the ribs and went off to collect everyone. I swear, I was going to be black and blue before this wedding affair was over.

TWENTY-ONE

I awaited while people and dogs populated the car. It took a minute for the seating arrangements to be worked out between four legs and two. Lily surprised me—and I think Maddie, too—when she let her Max sit up front with us.

I winked into the mirror before heading off. Lily rewarded me with a wink and a grin. So the little devil was spying on Maddie and Max. I should have known, and now I was a part of her conspiracy. The grin stayed with me all the way down the street.

"Where are we going, Uncle Jim?" Lily asked.

I looked across at Maddie, as though welcoming her into my conspiracy. "Oh, I don't know. I wanted to get away for a bit, is all. Maybe we can stop for ice cream and contemplate life before going back to the wedding madness."

"Ice cream sounds good. Right Zelda? Max, would you like some ice cream? Zoe likes ice cream."

"Jim does, too, Lily. I think a little too much, judging by his waistline," Maddie told her.

I broke into song. *"I scream. You scream. We all scream for ice cream."* Well, okay, it wasn't a song as much as a chant. The dogs barked. The women giggled. I basked in the affection, like the old dog that I was, happy knowing I'd reconnected with Zelda and Lily and Zoe and everyone else. As if to confirm it, a cold nose nuzzled my neck from the back seat.

"Lily. Is that you? Your nose is awfully cold. Are you sure you need ice cream?"

Lily's admonishment came fast. "Uncle Jim. That was Zelda. Bad girl, Zelda."

As if to reassure me, the old girl hit my neck a second time and I couldn't hold back the laughter. We caught a light right beside a building covered in plate glass. Human eyes in the car turned to check the reflection. I think even the dogs looked.

"Well, don't you all look like peas in a pod. What could be better than this, ladies and dogs? We have sun. We have blue sky. We have a cool breeze. Life is good. Right?"

"Life is good, Uncle Jim. We all think so," Lily confirmed for all of us.

Zelda, sitting in the back, woofed approval. I hit motel row and slowed. Maddie and I allowed our eyes to roam both sides of the street. I think we spotted the SUV at the same instant. "That's it."

An ice cream parlor lurked across the street, only a couple of buildings down. Sight-lines were good. There was cover if we chose the right table. I turned into the parking lot and Maddie was first out.

"I don't think they'll let dogs in, Lily," she said.

"Uncle Jim. Look. The sign says they have ice cream for dogs. How are we going to get ice cream for everyone?" she worried.

"I'm not sure. Maybe the owner has a solution. What do you think?"

He did, and we ended up with three small bowls and three cones and everyone was happy. We watched the dogs chase their ice cream bowls across the parking lot. Zoe nudged Zelda a couple of times, as though leading Zelda to her bowl.

I elbowed Maddie. "Did you see that?"

She only nodded. We sat in the shade and laughed at the dogs' antics and licked away to make short work of our own ice cream before a sun beating down in growing heat melted everything.

Tears rolled down Maddie's cheeks at the antics of the dogs. She called to Friday. He stopped and perked up his ears. Maddie walked over, picked up his ice cream bowl, and collected the others. It was doggie disappointment all-round until she returned the ice cream to the ground.

"Come on, dog people. Use geometry." She placed the bowls in a triangle and once again Zoe nudged Zelda into position over a bowl. They happily dug in without having to chase ice cream across the lot. Three white-mustachioed dogs looked our way, and I swear they smiled as tongues licked at ice cream mustaches.

"Come with me, you three. You need water."

They bounded after Maddie. Lily looked across the table and grinned. "I think Maddie likes our dogs."

"Did you ever have any doubt?" I asked her.

"Not any more, Uncle Jim."

I wanted to ask Lily about Zelda, but we were having such a good time. I didn't want to spoil it.

TWENTY-TWO

I recognized the man closing the door to the motel room. He was one of the two that visited the marina yesterday. "That's one of them across the street, Maddie."

Lily's eyes widened. "Uncle Jim. Did you bring us on a secret mission? Are we doing a stakeout?"

The man looked around the motel parking lot. He recognized a small car and waved. A woman I didn't recognize got out.

"That's the reporter. She was asking my dad and Warren all those questions," Lily said.

"Are you sure?"

"Oh yes, I'm sure. It's the same cute little car. I went to our parking lot to look at it."

"Now we know. Good job, Lily. There'll be a little something extra in this week's allowance for you."

Lily shielded her eyes and squinted while looking up at me. "I don't get an allowance, Uncle Jim. I work at the marina to earn spending money. James does, too. He had to work today. That's why he couldn't come for ice cream."

"In that case, I'll be talking to your mom and dad about a little raise this week to fatten up that pay envelope. We'll take James tomorrow. Do you think that would be all right?"

"I guess so. Why are we checking that woman out? Are we spying on her? Did you bring us on a stakeout? Are we on a secret assignment? Did I break the case? Do we need a secret signal to tell everyone we're all right?"

The words tumbled out of Lily's mouth and my first thought was that she was watching too much television. It had to be the most exciting thing she'd done in a while. I looked at Maddie, hoping she'd take the initiative and cool Lily's jets. It wasn't to be.

"You know, Lily, sometimes we have to do things and we don't know why. This is one of those times. I don't know what's up, but now I have more information to add to the picture, thanks to you," Maddie told the girl.

"That's what my mom used to say when we were in Florida before I found Zelda and you and Allie rescued us."

Maddie went into thought as Lily's revelation added more information to the puzzle concerning my circle of friends. I think she was finding it all a little overwhelming.

"Do you have questions, Maddie? Now is the time."

"I think I'd like to know how Lily met Zelda."

Lily was okay with that. "Then will you tell me where you found Max?"

"You bet I will. Who's going first?" Maddie asked.

I herded the dogs into the shade under the umbrella and went for more ice cream. I didn't hear any complaints, and by the time I returned, Maddie was completely engrossed in Lily's tale. Lily only stopped talking long enough to spoon ice cream into her mouth. Finally, she halted, breathless and excited. "All right, Maddie. It's your turn."

"My goodness. That was some story, Lily. Your Uncle Jim must have had his hands full to get you and your mom to safety."

"My dad died, and we were in the van. You know. Living in it. And then Zelda—but I already told you all that," she said.

Maddie took a breath and looked across the parking lot. I followed her gaze. The feds were gone, and so was our chance to follow them. Max settled in beside Lily, hoping to get a lick in on her ice cream. Zelda did the same, nuzzling my thigh and then, wanting to make sure she had my attention, she snorted. Instead of more ice cream, I scratched her. She rested her muzzle on my leg and looked up with sad brown eyes.

I never could resist a brown-eyed girl. I dipped a paddle into the ice cream and Zelda licked to her heart's content.

"Let's see—"

Zoe must have felt sorry for Maddie now that Lily had taken over Max. In any case, Zoe was busy snuffling and poking and snorting until Maddie absentmindedly handed over a paddle for the dog to lick. Not content with that, Zoe sidled up to Maddie and kept leaning against her leg until a stray hand found an ear and the dog was happy.

"I think Zoe has adopted you, Maddie."

"I think you're right, Jim. I don't mind. I like her, too."

Maddie hesitated before smiling at Lily. She was getting ready to dive in and tell her how she ended up with Lilly's Max and her Friday.

I was left to wonder why it took three feds to put their effort into Warren and Hank. The so-called reporter was obviously one of them. Was there a reason Maddie and I had been detained on our way here?

I was starting to think we would be next in line for a visit.

TWENTY-THREE

The feds were out of sight but not out of mind. I sat back, anticipating Maddie's tale. Zelda was going to have to be happy with ear-scratching and petting. No way was I going to miss this to make another ice cream run.

"So you want to know how I ended up with your dog. Very well."

Maddie hesitated, I suspect more for effect than anything. Lily stared and waited with bated breath. She was petting up a storm with her Max, who was basking in the little girl's long-lost affection like the ham he was.

"It was a year or maybe a little more. I was driving across the panhandle. I had just left my boyfriend of the past two years for good." Maddie looked across the table at me. "Don't ask why. That's another story."

She went on.

"I needed a break, so I pulled into a rest area. I don't like to stop around strange vehicles when I'm traveling. I drove past all the cars to the end of the parking area. There was no one there."

She halted, remembering.

"Where was I? Oh yeah. I stopped. It was hotter than blazes. Went in and did my business and then hit up the vending machine for a couple of water bottles for the drive."

Lily's elbows were on the table. Her chin rested on her hands. She was intent on listening to Maddie's story.

Maddie took a breath and went on. "For some reason, I looked back. I discovered a big black dog following me to the car. His tail was wagging furiously. He was panting. So I tipped the bottle into my hand and let him have some water. He finished and snorted and woofed and followed me the rest of the way to the car."

She paused to wait for encouragement from Lily.

"Then what happened?" Lily was still staring intently at Maddie.

She smiled at the girl. "Well, he plopped down on his rear at my driver's door. I couldn't open it. He wouldn't move. I went around to open the passenger door. I wanted to get back on the road. I didn't want to wait for a stubborn dog to move out of my way. He wasn't blocking the car. He was in the way of the door. He wouldn't let me open it."

"What happened when you opened the other door?" Lily wanted to know.

"I didn't spot the devil until he was scrambling past my legs. He jumped into the passenger seat and sat down. He didn't even call shotgun."

Lily laughed. "Oh Max, you are a sly one, aren't you?"

"I looked for a tag. He didn't have a collar. Nothing. I called out for anyone who'd lost a dog. No one answered. No one seemed to be searching for a lost dog. I couldn't leave him there. I just couldn't, not in the heat, without water. And to top it off, it was Friday, thus the name."

I nudged Lily. "It's a good thing it wasn't Saturday, right Lily?"

"Or Wednesday, Uncle Jim," she giggled. "We all thought he ran away. Or got tired of all of us. Or maybe someone dog-napped him."

"I don't know about that, Lily. But I've had him for about a year. I bought some books and spent time training him to recognize my hand signals. And then I met Jim. And he took him to a vet because I didn't know when the dog had last been to see one."

"That's when we found the tag, Lily. It was during Friday's visit to Dr. Hannah," I told her.. "She scanned him for the microchip."

"I'm glad you did. I was worried he was out somewhere all alone with no one to love him."

"Well, I love him," Maddie assured the girl. "And now you have him back to love even more."

The black SUV pulled into the motel parking lot across the street.

"Ladies, we have our subjects back. It's secret agent time."

"See, Maddie? We are secret agents. I can't wait to tell James all about it."

TWENTY-FOUR

It didn't take long to become bored watching cars across the road from the ice cream shop's patio. It was getting hot. The dogs were panting. I put the top up on the convertible and turned on the air. Lily called shotgun and Max jumped in and stole the space between us.

Maddie and Zelda and Zoe shared the back. Somehow, Zelda managed to get caught on the wrong side of the back seat. She scrambled over Maddie's lap and edged Zoe out of her seat directly behind me. To show me who was still boss, Zelda did her thing and planted a cold nose against the back of my neck.

"Bad girl, Zelda." Of course, Zelda had to do it again, and we all laughed as I pulled into the street and headed for the marina.

The SUV charged out of the motel's parking lot and took up a position several car lengths behind. We'd been made. I didn't tell Maddie, but only because I didn't want to alarm Lily. It took a moment before I changed my mind. Lily would have to know she was still in on her secret agent mission.

"Someone from the motel is following us. I'm expecting to get pulled over. If it comes to that, you're going to have to control the dogs. Understand, Lily?"

"Oh yes, Uncle Jim. I'll take care of them. They listen to me. I'll make them stay. They listen to James, too," she added, probably because I told her he could come with us tomorrow.

"It's important, Lily. You really have to control them, no matter what happens. And here's the lights."

Maddie and Lily turned around to look. "Blue lights," Lily announced. "Are you going to stop, Uncle Jim?"

"I have to, Lily. It's the law," I told her.

"All right. I'll look after the dogs." Lily began talking to Max beside her, and then to the dogs in the back. Zelda and Zoe perked up their ears and even Maddie paid attention. I know because she winked at me in the mirror.

To get out of traffic, I turned in at the first mini-mall and shut off the engine. "Lily, put your hands on the dashboard. Do exactly what the nice policeman says. You know the drill, Maddie."

I gripped the wheel and wondered why they were putting us through this exercise in futility.

Lily called to the dogs. "Max. Zelda. Zoe." Dog ears perked up on hearing Lily's commanding tone. "Sit. Stay."

As though their ears were riveted to the girl's voice, they did exactly that. No snuffling. No shifting. No barking. Tails stopped wagging. "Good girl, Zelda, Good girl, Zoe. Good boy, Max."

It was all she had time to say.

"Sir, would you step out of the car?"

I had one last thing to say to Lily and Maddie, but it was mostly for Lily's sake. "Ladies, keep your hands in plain sight, on the dash or the seat back, okay?

I rolled my eyes at Maddie in the mirror and got out. I made sure to keep my own hands in sight. "Is there something you need, boys? My friends and I just floated a vat of ice cream and we need to get home to use the facilities."

The agent pulled aside his jacket to float the piece on his hip. Maybe he wished he'd had time for ice cream, too. "There's no need for that. You know who I am. In fact, you know who everyone is, don't you?" I didn't give him a chance to get a word out. "In fact, your little reporter trick a couple of days ago didn't go so well, did it? I heard she didn't get so much as a yes or no for her troubles."

An eye ticked, giving the cop away.

"Yeah, I thought so. I spotted her across from the ice cream shop. You never figured on that. If it wasn't for the huge vehicles you types like to parade around in, I would never have seen her in that mini-car. And just so you know, it was the little girl sitting in the front seat that made her."

I stopped there. I still wasn't sure what they wanted with us. Perhaps they wanted to intimidate us. That wasn't going so good, though. I was quite pleased with myself. "So then, if there's nothing you want, and if you're finished intimidating women and children and three dogs, I'll be on my way. It's that, or tell us why we're being detained."

In the background, I heard Maddie chuckle. "The dogs won't talk. Any one of the humans might if you sweat us hard enough. I'd start with Lily, the girl in the front seat. She's the youngest and the most vulnerable."

Maddie's chuckle turned into a loud laugh. Even Lily was giggling. The uncomfortable red face in front of me backed off and turned to walk back to his giant vehicle and its blinking blues.

"Can I get back in my car now, agent? Are we free to go," I called after him. I waited for him to climb in and pull out into traffic.

"That went rather well even if I do say so myself. Let's get home. What do you say to that, girls and dogs?"

Lily took it all in stride. "Uncle Jim, I would never break under questioning," she assured me in a solemn voice. "I learned that from TV. And now we all know our secret *Okay* sign, too."

I think she was pleased as punch knowing she had been on a stakeout with her Uncle Jim and Aunt Maddie. Lily got out of the car, held a finger to her lips, and did a *Shh* as soon as we got home. Girl and dogs scrambled out of the car together.

I couldn't fault Lily for a thing.

TWENTY-FIVE

Our impromptu ice cream party would have been a success but for getting pulled over by federal agents. It was a form of threat. That Lily was in the car when they did it annoyed me to no end. She certainly wasn't involved in anything. It didn't put me in a good frame of mind.

My crew scattered as soon as I pulled into the marina lot. I made for the dock, hoping to find Warren. I had plenty of questions now that I knew the reporter he'd warned me about was working with the feds, or more likely, for them. I found both Warren and Hank, a bonus.

"Are you two going to tell me what the hell is going on? Or am I going to have to sweat it out of you? Little Lily was with us when we were pulled over after we left the ice cream parlor. They were in the motel lot across the street with the reporter impostor.

The men exchanged worried glances. I kept going. "You already know Maddie and I were shanghaied in that excuse for a town. I witnessed your argument with those men on the wharf. I texted the plate on the SUV in the parking lot to a cop in the big city."

I was going for the fear factor. I fired off the questions as fast as I could, and I didn't want to be interrupted. "When the results come back, what three-letter agency is it going to be? ATF? DEA? Something else? What's going on? Who wants to be the first to spill the beans?"

Warren looked down at the ground like a guilty person before replying. "The ATF—"

Hank held up a hand. "Warren. We were told not to or else."

"I don't care. They've been hassling us for weeks, Hank. It's gone on long enough. It's time Jim knew. He's in the middle of it anyway."

"If Allie finds out, or Erica, we'll both be in trouble, and you know it," Hank said.

I couldn't believe what I was hearing. "You two better come with me. The trailer is a better place for the discussion we're about to have." Warren and Hank followed me up the hill. "You two wouldn't know, but I'm this far from telling Allie what I know, and what I suspect. If she wasn't as big as a house, I'd have told her already. So like I asked, who wants to be first?"

Allie chose that moment to begin climbing the hill. Given her advanced state of pregnancy, she wasn't in a hurry. It took effort, but she made it under duress. "Who's as big as a house? If you know what's good for you, Nash, you'll keep it to yourself."

A very pregnant Allie waddled to a chair, released a long sigh, and sat down. "Ohh, that feels so good. My back is killing me."

Warren appeared relieved his fiancée appeared. He couldn't be forced to tell more. "Are you sure you're going to make it to our wedding day, honey? Maybe we should do it early, just in case."

"Not on your life. It's in two days or nothing. And you can take that to the minister. Are you guys coming down to join us?"

"We'll be there in a few minutes, Allie. I've been trading war stories with the menfolk," I said.

"Well, the menfolk better get their butts in gear or the

womenfolk will have words to share. All right?" Allie pushed herself out of the chair and groaned. I'm never doing this again, Warren."

"I told you, dear. You do the first nine months and I'll do the next five years.

I was pretty certain Warren was nuts to promise that, but what did I know about raising a kid? I could barely look after myself. I'd even farmed the care of Zelda out to Lily and James.

"You're a good man, Warren. I could never do it," I told him.

Hank had his own experience to relate. "I'm doing it now with my adopted daughter and son, and they're a lot older. I'm thinking Warren is going to eat those words after sitting up nights for a month with a crying baby."

Allie smiled like an angel and struggled down the hill. I waited until she was at the bottom and out of hearing range.

"All right, you two. It's time," I said.

Hank began reluctantly. "It's the ATF. They want us to run guns for them."

"What? Say that again. Run guns to who?" I was incredulous.

"To boats offshore. They won't tell us more than that."

"It has to be Mexico," I said.

"Most likely. We keep telling them no. They don't take no for an answer. They're threatening to seize the business if we don't do as they ask. Except it's gone beyond asking. They're telling us what to do."

"And those were the two on the dock?" I needed confirmation.

"Yes. Those two," Warren confirmed.

I told them what we witnessed earlier. "The reporter is one of them. I caught them meeting at the motel across from the ice cream parlor. They must have found out somehow that I was showing up. Why else would we have been hauled off to a small-town jail?"

"Could be. We don't know what to do, Jim. The pressure is getting to us. If Allie finds out we're doing their bidding, she'll kill us."

"That better not be the only reason you're playing hard to get," I said.

"It isn't. But it's a pretty good one."

"You two go down and join the rest of them. I'm going to stay up here and think on it for a bit. If they ask, tell them I'll be down in a while."

It wasn't long before all three dogs showed up to help me watch the sun setting over the bay. Zelda took up her familiar position, and Friday and Zoe were on either side of her.

The dogs were good company, but I couldn't ask them for advice. I had to come up with a solution all by myself.

TWENTY-SIX

I left Maddie in the trailer and took my spot on the ground with my back against the tree. A gentle breeze played a song on the leaves. It wasn't long before good old Zelda ambled up the hill to sit with me. I stroked her neck and scratched at an ear. She sighed and looked at me.

"Do you miss Lucy, Zelda? Do you miss her?"

Zelda's ears perked up at the sound of the woman's name.

"I know, Zelda. You miss Lucy too. I'm sorry. It's my fault."

As though in sympathy, Zelda nuzzled me with her cold nose. She snuffled and stretched out, resting against my outstretched legs. We looked out over the water together, as though expecting someone, anyone, to show up.

"Lucy isn't coming back, Zelda. She's gone for good."

Zelda snuffled and Maddie chose that instant to join us on the grass. "I thought I heard you out here. What are you two old dogs talking about under the shade tree?"

"We were just having words about an old friend. I think she still misses her. Her ears perked up when I said her name."

Zoe and Friday trotted up the hill with Lily and James

in tow to join me. "Hi Uncle Jim. I'm sorry I missed the stakeout. I was working," James said.

Lily looked at me and held a finger to her lips. I figured they shared secrets. I didn't admonish her.

"You did, but it wasn't intentional. It was more by accident that it became a stakeout. We stopped for ice cream, and there they were, across the street. Tomorrow on your day off you and I are going for ice cream."

"Can we bring Zelda? Did you miss her when you were away? I've been looking after her like you asked. Lily helps me take care of her, too.

"You've been doing a good job with Zelda, James. You too, Lily. It seems even Zoe looks out for her."

Lily and James exchanged glances. I pretended not to notice. James went on. "Zelda likes coming up here to be under the tree in the evening. She looks out over the water like she's waiting for someone. When it starts to get dark, Zoe comes up and they come home together."

"I explained to Zelda just a few minutes ago. That's my fault. The person she's waiting for won't be coming back." I didn't want to say Lucy's name, probably as much for me as for Zelda.

"Are you going to take Zelda with you when you go home?" James asked. "Max could take care of her like Zoe does."

I looked at him, surprised he would think that. "No, James. I won't be taking Zelda. She's pretty happy here, don't you think? Zelda wouldn't like the noisy city. She likes you and Lily. And Zoe is good company for her. I see how Zoe takes care of her, too. Now that Max is back, Zelda has him for another good friend."

There was almost an audible sigh shared by Lily and James. James cheered up considerably. I think Lily was wondering, too, because she seemed to relax as well.

"Are you happy to hear that?"

Two nodding heads gave me my answer.

"Good. I know Zelda needs you both."

I got the impression Lily and James were two peas in the same pod. They seemed to get along well. They both liked the dogs and the dogs liked them. They were earning their allowance by doing chores around the marina. I was satisfied I found a good home for Kara's son, James, with Erica, the woman's sister. I couldn't be happier for them.

"I'm going to sit here with Maddie for a while. Maybe the dogs will stay, too. Why don't you go down and ask everyone if they'd like Uncle Jim to pick up some takeout? I do requests."

The kids wandered off and the dogs stayed behind. I got the feeling Zoe and Max were showing support for their wistful friend and mother, Zelda. She really did miss Lucy. I sighed, and Zelda sighed, and Maddie stood up.

"You four are turning into a pity party," she said.

"Get back down here. You're part of the family now, like it or not."

"I'll get some water for the old dogs under the tree. Don't go anywhere. I'll be right back."

I was feeling sorry for myself, and Maddie knew it. The dogs sensed it and sympathized, too. "I'll have a ginger ale if you can find one. Are you going to come with us tomorrow?" I hoped she would.

"I wouldn't miss it for the world," she assured me.

TWENTY-SEVEN

Maddie and **I** stepped out of the trailer into bright sunshine and growing late-morning heat. The humidity would come later. James and the dogs waited patiently in the shade beneath the tree.

"Let's get a move on, dogs and people. We're burning daylight." I was pretty sure James knew it was my fault I was late, and obviously not his.

"We're ready, Uncle Jim. Zelda wanted to wake you up, but I wouldn't let her."

I smiled down at James and messed his hair. Zelda huffed and woofed and nosed my legs. She sensed a car ride and wanted to get me moving in the right direction.

"Look who wants to go for a car ride." When we were together, Zelda was always ready to jump in. Front or back, it didn't matter as long as she could stick her head out the window—after she bumped my neck with her cold nose, that is.

Zelda woofed again and James called shotgun for Max to get up front while he jumped in the back with Zelda and Zoe.

"I have a sneaking suspicion you're being spied on, dear. Lily isn't the only one."

"Oh, I suspected it since I arrived with Friday. It's all

right. I don't mind. I'm kind of enjoying it, actually. It's fun. But don't you dare tell them I'm on to them, shamus."

I crossed my heart and put a finger to my lips.

"Who wants the top down?" I called out.

Everyone barked but the people. I lowered the top, powered down the windows, and we were off. In back, doggie heads hung out of the car. In the mirror, I spotted the male passenger grinning like a banshee. "Are you enjoying yourself, James?"

"I sure am. I couldn't have a better day off, Uncle Jim. Do you think I could talk my dad into getting a car like this?"

I pretended not to notice his dad remark. I was secretly glad James settled in with his aunt and Hank. "Well, it never hurts to ask," I said. "Maybe when you get a little older I could put in a good word for you." He seemed satisfied with that.

I pulled into the ice cream parlor and dogs and people headed for the window. The dogs, after their feast yesterday, knew the way and beat us to it.

"I don't think I've ever had ice cream in the morning, Uncle Jim."

I smiled at the boy. "Well, your mom and dad don't need to know everything, do they, James? As a responsible adult, I say we put the blame squarely the dogs."

That got me a dirty look from Maddie and a great big grin from the boy. "I won't tell." He placed a finger to his lips and made the same *Shh* Lily made.

"Vanilla for the dogs," I called. "The two-legged variety can have whatever you want."

James laughed and reached into his pocket. His hand came out with a twenty. "My treat, everyone," he called to us.

A surprised Maddie wouldn't allow it. "James. You

don't have to do that. It's our treat since you couldn't come yesterday."

"But I want to. This is why I get an allowance. Well, it's not an allowance. I get paid for chores. I can spend it on whatever I want."

"You work hard for it. Let us treat you. You weren't able to be here yesterday."

Reluctantly, James replaced the money in his pocket. "Okay, but don't tell Lily how cheap I was."

Maddie mouthed her own *Shh,* and James grinned at her. "We won't, I promise."

The rest of them returned to the benches beneath the umbrella. I ordered last and on my walk to join them, I looked across the street to check out the motel. I called to Maddie. "Is that Hank's car over there?"

She shaded her eyes for a look. James was busy putting out the bowls for the dogs.

"I'm not sure. Oh, wait. You're right."

Hank exited the car and hurried toward a room. What was he doing there? Was he on his way to finalizing a deal of some sort? I didn't see Warren. He had to be out of the loop.

"Something isn't right. I'm going across the street. Keep James and the dogs here, please."

Zelda made to follow me across the street. Maddie called to her, but just like a woman with a mind of her own, Zelda wouldn't listen. I halted at the curb and knelt beside Zelda. "Zelda."

Her ears perked up. "You're too old to be crossing the street without a leash. Go back and sit with James. Now. Zelda, go to James."

She stuck a cold ice-cream nose against my chin and let out an annoyed snort before hanging her head. Stubborn as she was, she sat down and wouldn't move. I pretended I didn't notice Zoe come for her. She gave Zelda a nudge with her nose and Zelda got up on all fours.

"Good girl, Zelda. Go with Zoe."

I waited for Zoe to lead Zelda back to the fold. The old girl turned her head to me, but she ended up waddling in the direction of the waiting ice cream bowl she deserted to be with me.

James called to her, and both dogs quickened their pace. Good girl, Zelda. Your ice cream is waiting."

I waited for a break in traffic and crossed the street. I took a look in Hank's unlocked car. It offered no clues. I approached the door to the room and listened. Muted voices. Two men and a woman. I couldn't make out anything. No one was yelling this time. Perhaps Hank had reconciled himself to accepting the obvious and was going along with whatever they wanted.

On the other hand, I wasn't satisfied in the slightest. I retraced my steps and rejoined the ice cream party. Zelda's wet nose found my hand, as though saying, *See, I could have gone with you after all.* I reached to scratch beneath her chin and I think she almost grinned.

Zelda is glad you came back, Uncle Jim. She follows you everywhere."

"Well, we do have a past, James. I missed her something awful when I asked you to take care of her. I didn't know if I'd ever see her again. I kind of like sitting with her under the tree. It's cool and quiet there in the evening. I talk out my troubles and she listens and every once in a while she pokes me with a wet nose to let me know she cares."

James went all serious. "Are you sure you won't be taking Zelda when you leave? I know you already said no, but—"

I didn't hesitate. I didn't want him to think I was considering it. Especially now if what I suspected about Zelda was true. "No. Zelda is your dog now, James. We're just renewing our acquaintance. I'm enjoying spending time with her again after all these years."

"It's nice to see you sitting with her under the tree," he said. "She's always there in the evening when it gets cool. Lily and I always go up there with her. Now that you're back, we let you spend time with her."

It was the second time I saw James almost rejoice, knowing I wouldn't be taking Zelda with me.

"Zelda made me feel at home when I first came here," James explained. "On school days she would walk me to the end of the driveway and watch until I got on the bus. When it was time to be home, she was always waiting for me in the same place. I was so happy to see her. Her tail would wag and she'd woof and snort and we'd walk home together. She really helped me. Lily did, too."

"Did I ever tell you how I met Zelda?" I asked.

Maddie pretended she didn't hear, but I wasn't fooled. Her ears perked up, kind of like Zelda's did when I mentioned Lucy.

TWENTY-EIGHT

I still didn't know what I was going to do about the feds encroaching on Allie's business. Spotting Hank on his own visiting the hotel told me Warren had been left out of the loop. Hank must have realized that Warren would keep me apprised of the situation against his wishes.

While it really wasn't any of my business, my curiosity had been piqued. The shouting match I witnessed on the wharf couldn't be good, seeing as how it was going down on Allie's wedding weekend.

Hank had his problems with drugs in the past. His addiction almost cost him the family business. He got through it thanks to his sister, Allie. She brought me in. I convinced him doing back-to-backs in rehab would cure his ills, although I suppose it came to more than that. I never let on to Allie. All that mattered was that the man finally got clean.

I wanted to bide my time and wait for the right moment to confront Hank and Warren. I figured both of them needed the pep-talk, seeing as how Warren was about to become part of the family. The problem was, I didn't know what my pep talk should entail.

Warren was avoiding me. I suppose he was within his

rights, seeing as how he might think he was stealing Allie away from me. The truth was, Allie and I parted company a long time ago. He even sent me the rings in the big city to get them properly engraved, for crying out loud. I was happy for the guy. I was happy for both of them.

Reluctant as Maddie was to accompany me to the wedding, she could see that whatever Allie and I once had was over. I was glad Allie pulled her aside and cleared the air.

At least, that's what I assumed they talked about, since Maddie ended up staying in the trailer. She ended up volunteering to take on some of Allie's wedding duties, too. Given that the poor woman was due any day, she was grateful. If Allie made it to her wedding day without giving birth, I'd be surprised.

So here I was, back at square one. I loaded the crew into the car for the ride home. "Did everyone get enough ice cream?" From the back seat, a cold nose hit my neck as I knew it would. "James. Was that you? Is that your way of saying you want more?"

Zelda traded her nose for her tongue and licked my ear. James laughed. A smiling Maddie took my hand in hers.

"No, Uncle Jim. That was our Zelda."

We all laughed. I took us home and wandered down to the dock to see what I could see.

TWENTY-NINE

I found Warren at the end of the wharf, swabbing the deck on a company sailboat. He whistled a random tune to the back-and-forth motion of the mop. He saw me approaching and waved. "How was the ice cream?"

"Everybody seemed happy to get there and happy to leave with full stomachs. You know, you can pay someone to do that."

Warren dipped the mop into the bucket. "Well, I suppose the business could, but it keeps me humble. Lily and James don't need to be cleaning up someone's puke, even if they are getting an allowance to do it."

"You've come a long way, old friend. Who would have known all those years ago when Allie commented on your abs." I grinned up at him. "You didn't know then, of course. Did she ever tell you?"

I always wondered if she had.

"No, she didn't. Is there a story there you shouldn't be telling?"

"Yes, there is, and no, not now. I'm going to wait until my best-man speech," I warned him.

"I could cancel that," he said.

"You could, but then you'd have to deal with the wrath of Allie. And probably Erica and Maddie by now, don't you know? Plus, I still have the rings somewhere in the trailer."

"Yeah. I noticed the women didn't waste time bonding with your latest. That's a good thing as far as I'm concerned."

"You don't know how close it was, Warren. I was phone shopping for a hotel when Maddie finally conceded and told me she'd stay in the trailer."

"Surely you know by now Allie can talk anyone into doing what she wants. She does it in such a nice way most people don't even realize it."

I had to agree. I knew from experience with the woman.

"You know Maddie is going to be maid of honor, right?" Warren said.

It was my turn to be surprised. Strange that she hadn't mentioned it. "Well. Now I know. I must be out of the loop. That's why she's been taking the car and sneaking off. I was worried she'd found someone with better abs than mine."

Warren finished his deck swabbing and stepped onto the dock. I couldn't put it off any longer. I didn't want to belabor the point, considering we'd already talked it out. "Are you sure there's nothing else going on with the feds? You didn't leave anything out, did you? Those men—"

"What men?"

Warren's ears were tuned in now, and I knew for sure there was something to it. "The two men you and Hank were arguing with the other day. During the breakfast. On the dock."

Did Warren think I was so dense I'd forgotten our talk? I waited for his reaction. It was long in coming as he looked out over the water. That seemed to be a thing here. The dogs did it, too.

"Oh, those two. Didn't we deal with that already? I'm going to have to ask Hank if it's all right to talk about it with you when he isn't around. It's his business."

"His and Allie's, both," I reminded him. "You'll no doubt join them in it at some point after the wedding. It's not wise to keep secrets from the people you love. Just ask me."

"I know. I remember how tight you were wound when Kara showed at the resort."

"So what are you going to do about it?" I asked him?

He considered before answering. "I left it to Hank to handle."

So that's why Hank was alone at the motel. "Is he capable of dealing with those types on his own?"

Warren looked surprised. "On his own? What do you mean? Who says they're feds, anyway?"

I just had it confirmed.

"It's my job, remember? Former big-city cop, now a private investigator. There's two of us here that fit half of that description. Maddie is a PI, too."

I waited, wanting him to think I knew more than I did. I was hoping he might reveal something I could use. "So what's going on? Do you want to tell me, or do you want to tell Allie?"

I hated doing it this way, but I had him. I also didn't want Allie to end up getting hurt in a business she had dug out of drug debt using her very own abilities. No thanks to her brother.

Warren, perhaps sensing my reluctance to board a sailboat, gestured for me to follow him to one of their cigarettes. Warren punched the button to engage the fans and waited before firing up the powerful engines. I cast off. He handed me a vest before donning his own and steering us past the breakwater. Once on the outside, he firewalled the throttles. Engines roared to life and propelled the bow to bang against the waves until he worked it onto the step.

We were off. Wind whistled past the cockpit, making

it difficult to talk, so I waited. Warren must have started to feel guilty. It wasn't long before he throttled back to a more reasonable speed. The roaring of the powerful engines quieted.

"Talk, Warren. We've been friends through thick and thin too long for you to clam up now. Especially when Allie's business is on the line."

Warren didn't look happy I'd shanghaied him, but he was the one who invited me out on the water. He had essentially shanghaied himself. "What's going on? What were those men doing?"

"They're feds. You already know that. ATF."

"What does the ATF want with the business?" I asked.

"They started coming around four or five weeks ago. I noticed people coming and going. Different cars. Those SUVs, too. Men and women. Dark glasses. They didn't look like foreigners. I didn't know what to make of it. One day when I was out taking a look—"

"So you went investigating on your own?" I asked.

"Yeah, well, I wanted to know who they were and why they were lined up to look over the business. With two kids running free-range you can't be sure any more, you know? The dogs were here, but Zelda is getting old. Zoe belongs to Lily and James, but she's only one dog."

I had to give him points for trying.

"I confronted them. That's when they flashed badges and loaded me into one of those black SUVs for a talk."

I was betting he didn't like what they had to say. I waited for him to go on.

"I was smart enough to tell Hank about it. He insisted that Allie not know. And before you jump on me, I know. I should have told her, but with the pregnancy and everything else, I didn't want to upset her. She works just as hard as the rest of us, harder perhaps. Too hard with a baby on the way. She won't stand down."

I wanted to tell the man he was a dumbass for not

telling the woman he was about to marry and would soon be having his child. I bit my tongue. I wanted him to keep talking. When he didn't, I pushed.

"What do they want, Warren?"

While I waited, I thought about everything in my past that led up to this moment. All the DEA bull crap I went through. A crooked agent. Dead agents. Work in Mexico. Mostly it did me no good, other than a fat payday at the end of it all. How would I get that through to Warren?

When he didn't respond, I pushed again.

"What did they offer? They must have offered something for your cooperation. What was it?"

"Climb aboard, Jim. It's time, I guess."

THIRTY

Warren punched the button to engage the fans and waited before firing up the powerful engines. I cast off. He handed me a vest before donning his own and steering us past the breakwater. Once on the outside, he firewalled the throttles. Engines roared to life and propelled the bow to bang against the waves until he worked it onto the step.

We were off. Wind whistled past the cockpit, making it difficult to talk, so I waited. Warren must have started to feel guilty. It wasn't long before he throttled back to a more reasonable speed. The roaring of the powerful engines quieted.

"Talk, Warren. We've been friends through thick and thin too long for you to clam up now. Especially when Allie's business is on the line."

Warren didn't look happy that I'd shanghaied him, but he was the one who invited me out on the water. He had essentially shanghaied himself. "What's going on? What were those men doing?"

"They're feds. You already know that. ATF."

"What does the ATF want with the business?" I asked.

"They started coming around four or five weeks ago. I noticed people coming and going. Different cars. Those

SUVs, too. Men and women. Dark glasses. They didn't look like foreigners. I didn't know what to make of it. One day when I was out taking a look—"

"So you went investigating on your own?" I asked.

"Yeah, well, I wanted to know who they were and why they were lined up to look over the business. With two kids running free-range you can't be sure any more, you know? The dogs were here, but Zelda is getting old. Zoe belongs to Lily and James, but she's only one dog."

I had to give him points for trying.

"I confronted them. That's when they flashed badges and loaded me into one of those black SUVs for a talk."

I was betting he didn't like what they had to say. I waited for him to go on.

"I was smart enough to tell Hank about it. He insisted that Allie not know. And before you jump on me, I know. I should have told her, but with the pregnancy and everything else, I didn't want to upset her. She works just as hard as the rest of us, harder perhaps. Too hard with a baby on the way. She won't stand down."

I wanted to tell the man he was a dumbass for not telling the woman he was about to marry and would soon be having his child. I bit my tongue. I wanted him to keep talking. When he didn't, I pushed.

"What do they want, Warren?"

While I waited, I thought about everything in my past that led up to this moment. All the DEA bull crap I went through. A crooked agent. Dead agents. Work in Mexico. Mostly it did me no good, other than a fat payday at the end of it all. How would I get that through to Warren?

When he didn't respond, I pushed again.

"What did they offer? They must have offered something for your cooperation. What was it?"

THIRTY-ONE

Warren ignored me. He pretended to fuss with the throttles before pushing them forward. He executed a wide turn and ended up aiming the cigarette for the breakwater. Nothing was resolved.

Allie was my concern. The baby was due any minute. If things went well, she'd be out of the hospital in a day or two, maybe a little longer. How long would Hank and Warren be able to put off the feds? If Warren was doing his job, he'd be there with Allie and the baby in the hospital.

Which meant Hank would be the one to do the deal. Was that why I'd seen him at the motel on his own? Why was he so hell-bent on meeting with the agents? Was time running out on a deadline?

But exactly what would the deal entail? The feds wouldn't tell me anything. In fact, they were probably a party to the chickenshit crap that went down when Maddie and I got hauled in. Who else but a showoff sheriff would throw people in jail without cause unless he was trying to make points with someone?

So there it was. I was back to Hank. And Erica. And Lily. And James. Allie, too. The business. Was Hank going to jeopardize everything a second time? And if he was, what were the feds holding over him? I had to find out before it was too late.

Then it came to me. Like a flash of lightning landing too close for comfort and with no warning. How they knew I'd be driving out to the wedding. How they knew to call in a favor with a podunk sheriff. Wanting to delay me long enough that they could pressure Hank to do their bidding. Knowing I'd never go along and would talk him out of it if I found out.

Because whoever was heading up this deal knew I'd get wind of it. Knew I'd never let Allie and Hank go for it. Knew I had the means to put a stop to it. Knew not to approach Allie.

Time was running out for everyone. The wedding was tomorrow. I didn't have time to finesse a deal. I'd be on the hook for my own deal. The feds wouldn't be happy to have me insert myself into their deal to make it mine.

Tough love. I was feted to be the tough part of it.

Now that I had a solution to my liking, I relaxed and enjoyed what was left of the boat ride. I helped Warren tie off and made for the trailer and the tree. I sat down, put my back against it, and waited for the usual suspects to show up.

Before long, Zelda waddled up the hill with her nose to the ground, sniffing at the flowers along the way.

"Hello, old girl. Coming up here to keep an eye on things, are you?"

I rubbed and scratched and allowed her to put her cold nose wherever she wanted. Her tail wagged furiously. She snuffled and nudged and scratched my leg with a paw and generally told me how much she missed me. I didn't mind. I missed her, too. I let her know with my own scratching and rubbing and petting and everything else I could do. She seemed satisfied, and settled in beside me on her stomach. Together we looked out over the bay.

After a suitable time, Zoe followed, as if to check up

on Zelda. Max trailed behind. They settled in beside the queen of the litter and mimicked her behavior.

"Well look at all the old dogs."

It was Maddie joining us, and I asked the question that had been bothering me for a while. "What do you make of Zelda? Do you think she's having trouble seeing?"

At the sound of her name, the dog nudged me. I acknowledged her by reaching for an ear and scratching, and she was happy.

"I didn't want to say anything. Perhaps Lily knows more. Or James. Why don't you ask them? They've been taking care of her. Maybe they didn't want to tell you. They know how much you love her."

It was true. I missed Zelda. I didn't know if it was because of Lucy and how I met the two of them. Then Maddie showed up with Friday and it filled two empty spots in my heart.

"Did I tell you how glad I am you're here?"

"Is this another pity party for old dogs and men?" she wanted to know.

"Maybe. Don't old dogs deserve pity and love?"

Before she could answer, Lily and James scurried up the hill. If I was going to ask, now would be the time. I jumped in with flailing arms and legs. "Lily, have you noticed anything strange about Zelda lately?"

Zelda's ears perked up when she heard her name. Lily looked at James with a guarded expression. I caught his nod of assent and waited. They both reached to pet Zelda before Lily responded.

"Well, Zelda is a good girl, Uncle Jim. You know that."

Zelda's tail flailed the grass on hearing Lily say her name.

"She misses you, but you know that," she added.

It was true. I missed Zelda just as much. As if to confirm it, Zelda met my hand with her cold, wet nose and snuffled. I rubbed her and she lowered her head.

"When she's in the house she moves really slow. She bumps into things sometimes. Not enough to hurt her, but still—"

James stretched out beside Zelda and began petting her. Her cold nose found his neck and he laughed and Zelda was content to find him beside her.

"We try not to move anything so she can find her way around. We want her to be safe. Everyone knows. We all look out for her. We all take care of her, Uncle Jim."

I scratched Zelda's neck, more for my own comfort, and she stretched out beside me like an old dog should, relaxed and comfortable in her own right.

"I noticed when we were having ice cream. She didn't find her bowl right away. Zoe helped her, didn't she?"

"Yes. Zoe takes the best care of her. She's always looking out for Zelda. James does too, Uncle Jim. So do I. Sometimes when it gets dark and Zelda hasn't come down the hill Zoe comes up to get her."

I could hardly talk. "She leads her."

"Yes."

My voice wavered. "Zelda has the best home ever with all of you to look out for her."

"Yes but we know she misses you."

"I miss her, too. Maybe she can stay in the trailer with us tonight. What do you think, Maddie? Would you mind?"

I looked around, but she already wandered off to the end of the dock. She was with Allie. The two women were deep in conversation.

THIRTY-TWO

I finally knew what I didn't want to know. Zelda was going blind. Of course she was. The poor girl had grown old missing the people she loved the most, and it was my fault.

It only made it worse when she followed Maddie to the bedroom. Zelda sat down at the head of the bed and stuck her head over, resting it on the mattress. She was checking to see if I was really there. It was something she used to do with Lucy when we were together.

"Are you two all right? Do I need to get her anything?" Maddie was trying to cheer me up.

"No, she'll be fine. She'll wander over to your side of the bed and do the same thing before the lights go out. If she can even see the light."

"In that case I'm flattered," she said.

"I might end up on your side of the bed, too," I told her.

But I didn't. Zelda came back to my side. I reached a hand to her and scratched and petted and she snuffled and finally settled on the floor. It was time to talk to Maddie about what was going on.

"I hear you're the maid of honor. Does that have anything to do with staying in the trailer?" Sheets rustled and she settled beside me in the dark. Zelda snuffled and I reached for her, wanting to reassure her.

"What's going on with the business, Jim? What do those men want?"

"Well, it's the ATF, so it must have something to do with arms. I don't think they want the outfit to run bootleg whiskey or cigarettes for them."

"Did Boyle ever get back to you about the plate on the SUV?"

I forgot about that. "He did. It's registered to a non-existent address in the city. Probably proceeds of crime. It's how feds end up with a lot of their vehicles."

"Why would they want the business? Who would they be running arms to?"

"The Mexicans," I told her.

But to what purpose? Mexico had more firearms than it could handle, and they were in the hands of the cartels. That included the police and the military. What's one more weapon when you already have more than you need?

It would have something to do with cash. Hard cash. Was someone on the take and wanting to use the marina business as a cover? Money laundering, perhaps.

I checked the time. Past midnight. Allie's wedding was today. Would I be able to come up with a solution to a problem she didn't know she had? And where would Warren and Hank fit into the equation?

I reached for Zelda. She nuzzled my hand, and, content that I was there for her, sighed and settled in beside the bed one more time. I was content that she was there for me, too.

THIRTY-THREE

Maddie slipped out of bed quietly, trying not to disturb me. That went out the window when the panic in her shrill voice came through.

"I have a million things to do. I can't sleep all morning."

I raised an eyelid. The bedroom was still dark until she flipped on a light. "Woman, it's not daylight. You're scaring Zelda. Worse, you're scaring me."

I reached to comfort Zelda and found her cold, wet nose. She gave me a lick in an attempt to do the same and we were mollified—a mutual admiration society of two. I pulled the covers over my head and wished I could do the same for Zelda. Then I remembered she probably couldn't recognize the light Maddie turned on.

"You might not want to stay in bed when you remember you have something to do before the magic happens."

What the heck was she going on about? I closed my eyes and lowered the covers. Already she was making for the shower. I mumbled and tried to ignore the commotion.

"The feds," she called to me. "Remember that? You're going to fix it. Or are you going NATO?"

What was this woman going on about now? "What does a defense treaty have anything to do with anything, especially a wedding?"

"NATO. *No action, talk only*. Get it in gear, buster. It's go time for you. Do you remember where you put the rings? Where's your good suit? Did you remember to bring it? Did you unpack it, or is it still sitting in your bag all wrinkled. Are your shoes shined? Did you bring a tie, at least? A white shirt? Do I have to do everything for you?"

"Would you like to aim the lamp in my eyes while you interrogate me like we're in a film noir?"

Following the third degree, Maddie hauled out my bag and hefted it onto the bed. "Just as I thought. I have to do everything around here. I swear, if stayed at home you'd be trying to fish wrinkled clothes out of a backpack with nothing in it."

"We'll go fishing later, honey."

I reached for Zelda again. "Good dog, Zelda. Don't let the crazy person upset you just because she's trying to upset me."

Maddie was doing a good job of that. It got even better when she came out of the shower and found me still in bed. "Nash. Get your rear end out of bed. It's time to greet the world. You don't have a tie. I checked."

The woman had no idea what time it was. She'd completely lost it. "There's no store open yet, Maddie. I'll get dressed and go pick one up just for you. What else do we need, now that you've got me going to a mall?"

"I don't need anything. It's you who needs a tie. Take Zelda with you. She'll enjoy the outing."

I wasn't so sure about that, although she did want to try crossing the street with me. Perhaps it would be good for her after all. It would give me an opportunity to see for myself how the dog's vision had deteriorated.

"Yes, dear. I'm on it," I assured Maddie.

But I wasn't. I was thinking about how I was going to get Hank and Warren out of their dilemma. With the wedding only hours away, I was going to have to—

"Maddie?"

"What now?" she almost screamed. She was obviously annoyed.

"When's the rehearsal?"

"There is no rehearsal. Allie is too exhausted and pregnant to have one. You should show up for the meetings instead of wandering off with kids and dogs for ice cream."

Hadn't she been there with me? Women. I'd never understand a one of them.

"Yes, dear. I understand."

Oftentimes I worked a lot of mileage from those four words. It seemed to work this time, too. Maddie opened the closet door and took out her maid of honor dress. It was stunning, and she wasn't even in it yet. Now the problem became one of telling her immediately, or later, when she had it on. I decided to keep my trap shut.

"Give me five more minutes. Zelda needs her sleep. She's old."

THIRTY-FOUR

I didn't hear the door slam. Or maybe I did. I couldn't remember. When next I checked the time, it was daylight-thirty and the mall would open in oh crap it was open. I ran through the shower. Found a bowl of food for Zelda. Watered her. Leashed up and walked her to do her business.

By the time we made it to the car, it was too close to noon and I was going to go down hard if I didn't get back in time to give the bride away. Zelda must have sensed I was running late, and she toddled along with nary a sniff or a snort to delay her, either.

Whatever was going on with the business and the feds would take a back seat when Maddie and Allie were finished with me if I showed up late for the wedding. Not to mention what Warren would do to his best man if I was a no-show.

I hurried Zelda back to the trailer. Changed into suit and pants and shirt and shoes. Checked my reflection in the mirror. Damn but I still had it. I would look good standing beside Maddie in her maid of honor dress. Provided I made the wedding, that is.

"Come on, Zelda. It's time. You're going to have to wait in the car. I know it's not proper. Maybe we'll figure something out on the way."

I ended up taking Zelda into the mall on her leash. To an onlooker she was a gray-muzzled, slow old dog waddling serenely along. She was a draw for the little ones as they screamed and pointed and tugged at their mothers' arms wanting a closer look. Zelda enjoyed the attention as she always did, and I didn't mind. I checked the time. Still plenty left to get to the wedding.

We located the store. I found a tie with the help of a salesman who took time to admire a regal Zelda. I let her sniff the tie and she smiled a doggie smile and allowed the salesman to stroke her neck and rub her ears.

"Good girl, Zelda. You picked out my tie. We need one for you now.

I spotted a fancy silk bandana. It was a perfect match for Maddie's maid of honor dress. I tied it around Zelda's neck and she shoved her cold nose under my chin and licked my neck.

"You are such a pretty girl, Zelda." She perked up and snuffled and held her tail high and pranced as much as the leash would allow. "You'll look so pretty beside Zoe and Max. You'll be the belle of the ball."

I paid and made for the exit. She pranced happily with me in tow.

"Lily and James are going to be surprised to see you in your new bandana. I wish Lucy was here to see you."

At the sound of the woman's name Zelda's ears perked up and she looked up at me. I knew immediately it was a mistake. Zelda's pace quickened and she pranced ahead as far as her leash would allow. She wanted to get home to see Lucy. I felt horrible knowing how disappointed Zelda was going to be.

We were on our way past the food court when I recognized them. They were leaning in, deep in muffled conversation. They didn't see me, but I saw them.

THIRTY-FIVE

I halted mid-step. Zelda kept going. She tugged at the leash, reluctant to be interrupted in her quest for home. I directed her to the food court, albeit a little slower than I wanted. I sat down with the duo and Zelda settled in beside me and nudged my thigh.

I knew right away I had the advantage when the two ATF men sat back and cursed me.

"Nash. What are you doing here? What do you want? Do you think that blind old dog is going to save your ass?"

I was good until they called Zelda old and blind. That they'd called her a dog didn't bother me. That's what she was. That they knew Zelda was blind told me they had the business under surveillance for quite a while.

"Gentlemen, you can insult me all you want, but I draw the line at calling my dog old and blind. Zelda could whip both your asses and all three of us know it."

Zelda chose that moment to bark nice and loud. It surprised the agents and they eyed her warily.

"See? Even she knows. Now here's what I know." I paused to be sure I had their attention. "I know you had me set up with that podunk police department in hillbilly heaven."

Their eyes widened but they remained silent. "Obviously, you had me under surveillance. I'm not stupid, gentlemen. Neither is Lily. You remember her, don't you? She's the little girl who made your agent posing as a reporter."

They looked at each other and turned red. "Yeah, I'd be embarrassed knowing that, too. Wait until it gets out. You'll be a laughingstock. I'm betting the emails will be flying with plenty of memes." I waited to let it sink in. "You had Allie's business under surveillance for quite a while."

They raised their hands to object.

"How stupid do you think I am? How else would you know Zelda was blind? Are you people so dense that you don't think other people are aware of what you're doing? Who's in charge of this op? Why do you want to use a business cover to run arms into Mexico? Who's on the take? Is it someone you know? Is it only the three of you? If that's the case, you've got to be awfully stupid to think you can get away with it."

Now they were paying attention.

"I'm sitting here to advise you to lay off Allie's business. Be sure to repeat that to your little lady, too. We all had a meeting and the decision was made to ignore you. You will go away, leave the business and the owners in peace forevermore, never to return."

That drew looks of incredulity that I'd been so audacious. "You heard right. Stay away. And you can tell Diana Holbrook I said so. *Capiche?*"

I swatted away a raised hand. "Listen to me. You will never set foot on that property again. If I ever find out you have, whether it's true or not, I'll reveal the names of every individual at the ATF, DEA, FBI and any other three-letter organization I can think of that I've ever worked with or for. I'll call in every favor I know and then some. And just so you know, I have plenty owing."

They sat back in their chairs, not yet comprehending.

"I'll reveal your names, too. I'll write reports. I'll talk to TV news. I'll call every reporter I know and talk. I'll talk so much they'll wish I never knew them." It was my turn to sit back in my chair. "Do. You. Understand?"

I didn't give them a chance to respond. Zelda and I had a wedding to attend.

"Come on, Zelda. It's time," I told her. She stood up, growled, and together we headed for the exit.

THIRTY-SIX

Zelda took the lead and we headed for the exit. She pranced ahead, knowing she was going home, stretching the leash as far as she could. I didn't call her to heel. At the car I knelt in front of her and ran my hand down her side. "Zelda, you are such a pretty girl with your bandana."

She licked my face. Her tail wagged furiously.

"You have to stay here. Zelda. Stay. I'll be back. Stay."

She sat on her haunches and licked my hand. I trotted off to retrace our steps in time to encounter the two agents. As I suspected, they were exiting the mall, on their way to following me to the car.

"Not so fast in that fancy suit, Nash. We have a wedding present for you."

The distance between them widened. I knew what was coming and I was prepared but for the damned suit jacket. I struggled to shed it, attempting to pull my arms free. The wasted effort forced them behind my back and I cursed. Sensing my vulnerability, number one moved in and swung for my gut. Breath exploded from my lungs and I doubled over.

The second punch was telegraphed like a navy

ensign waving signal flags. I lowered my head and braced my body for what I knew was coming. The fist connected and bounced off my skull. It hurt like hell but not as much as the hand that landed. I tore at the jacket restraining my arms and pulled it all the way on. Something ripped. I didn't care.

I drove a fist into a nose. A thick stream of blood ran down a chin. The agent shook his head to clear watering eyes and I kicked wildly at a kneecap. Unable to see through the tears streaming down his face, the man's punches went wild. I got off a second kick to a kneecap. It landed hard and he went down clutching at his injured hand.

Number two was the more practiced. He dodged and weaved and must have thought he was in a boxing match. I came up under a punch and landed a knee in his groin. He got busy doubling over and I landed a second knee into his gut. A sucking sound rewarded me and I rejoiced for only an instant.

Number one was back on his feet and spitting blood.

I dived in a second time with kicks. He caught a shoe and yanked it. I tried dealing him another foot and he took that shoe, too. I moved in on sock feet, wanting a quick end. Distracted by the shoes clutched in his hands, I managed a roundhouse kick and he dropped like a bag of rocks.

I returned to number two.

He was only just getting upright. He shook his head. Mumbled something. I slammed a fist against the side of his face and felt something break. For good measure, I aimed a sock-covered foot into his gut. A whoosh of air departed his lungs and took him down to join his partner already on the asphalt.

I straightened my tie as best I could, buttoned my jacket, and made for the car. Zelda was waiting patiently. I fed her a treat from my pocket.

"Good girl, pretty Zelda. It's time to go home."

I held the door for her and Zelda slowly jumped into the front seat. She sat up, looking proud and just as eager as when we left the mall. And why wouldn't she? We were going home.

THIRTY-SEVEN

I didn't have to look to see who was on the other end of the ringing phone. I put it on speaker and couldn't get a word in. Allie was too busy tearing me a new one.

"Jim? Where are you? We're waiting on you. If you're not here in five minutes, I swear—"

I used the hesitation to jump in. "We're on our way, Allie. Zelda and I will be right there. I had to go to the mall for a tie."

I pulled into the marina parking lot and the call went dead. Zelda followed me to the trailer. I pocketed the rings and made for the house with Zelda trotting after me. Allie met me at the door, where she regarded me with a shocked look.

"That's a pretty dress. It fits you perfectly. Where's Maddie?"

"Where did you find that tie? In a dumpster?"

"Now Allie. Zelda helped me pick it out. Check out Zelda's bandanna. It matches Maddie's maid of honor dress. Zelda picked it special just for you."

Zelda licked Allie's fingers. Distracted, she ignored the torn suit and my shoeless Joe look. Maybe she didn't notice. My socks were black.

"Thank you. We're all waiting, Jim. We're ready to go. Are you?"

"Of course. Wild horses couldn't keep us away, right, Zelda?"

I don't think Allie believed me, but I crooked my arm. Allie took it and I walked her toward the wharf to make our way to an anxious, waiting Warren. Three dogs pranced proudly after us. People I didn't know applauded. Much mumbling in the crowd assaulted my ears, but I figured it was because the woman on my arm was so beautiful and pregnant in her wedding dress.

A sunny blue sky looked down on the proceedings. I had the rings. What could go wrong? I handed off the bride and side-stepped to the beautiful maid of honor and grinned sheepishly.

"For crying out loud, Jim Nash. Where's your shoes? And look at your jacket. The sleeve is hanging off," Maddie admonished me. "It's a good thing you took Zelda with you or you'd still be wandering around in that mall."

"Did you notice her bandana? It matches your dress perfectly. She was so proud and happy when I tied it on for her."

"I saw. Zelda is the only one of you with the sense to get you here on time, isn't she?"

"Well—" I began, before Maddie cut me off.

"Stop talking and pay attention to the ceremony. I'll deal with you later. Good girl, pretty Zelda."

Zelda nudged our joined hands with a wet nose. I ruffled her ear. I hung my head and smiled sheepishly at Warren. He shook his head and grinned. When I had a chance to let him know his troubles were over, the man's grin would no doubt be a lot wider.

The service went off without a hitch. We were settling in to the meal when Warren tapped me on the shoulder. "Is your speech ready? It's your turn to bore everyone."

I reached into a torn pocket. The speech I spent so much time preparing was gone. "Of course. It's right here. Introduce me and I'll wow them with a paean to your magnificence."

Warren tapped a glass and the conversation in the small group quieted to a murmur and then silenced. "Everyone, I'd like to introduce Jim Nash, my best man. He's a little worse for wear, but still worth every nickel he spent in the mall doing some last-minute shopping for that flashy tie."

Laughter followed and I stood up. Tongue-tied in front of everyone, I hesitated for too long. Maddie nudged me. It was Zelda's cold nose on the back of my hand that brought me to my senses.

"Ladies and gentlemen and the rest of my fine, furry friends—" I began. "Warren, I'll have you know Zelda helped me pick out my tie." Laughter interrupted and I waited for it to subside. "Warren Jeffrey has been my good friend for what feels like forever. He helped me overcome a personal crisis in my life. He stood by me and wouldn't allow me to fall into a pit of despair, no matter how hard I tried."

I hesitated. "He picked me to be his best man, but I'm smart enough to know he's the better man—"

Allie stood up. Her chair tipped back and clattered onto the dock. "My water—?"

Wanting to be the perfect best man, I called out. "Will someone please get Warren's beautiful bride more water?"

"No. My water. It just broke. Get me to the car, Warren. It's time. Don't forget the bag. Come on honey, I can't wait another minute."

"Take her, Warren. I'll get the bag. Come on, Maddie. Hank. Erica. Lily. James. Zelda. Zoe. Max. Who did I forget?"

I had more than a full house in the Packard as we

chased after Warren and Allie.

"Can we put the top down, Uncle Jim?" James asked in all the excitement.

"I don't think we should do that while we're racing to a hospital. We might lose it." I powered down the windows instead. "You can all hang your heads out the window."

Allie's support group arrived minutes after she did. I let everyone off and they traipsed into the hospital, dogs and all, while I parked the Packard. I found them in a waiting room.

"How is she? Is Allie all right? How's the baby?"

"Everyone is fine. Warren is in with her. He promised he'd come out when he had news. We haven't seen him yet.

THIRTY-EIGHT

The wait for news went on. And on. And on. We talked and listened and told bad jokes and laughed. Did multiple commissary trips for terrible coffee. Ate snacks. Nurses tut-tutted the dogs. I was thankful no one asked us to leave, and was happy knowing that if anyone did, they'd be vastly outnumbered.

Finally, a pale-looking Warren in a wrinkled blue gown found us. "It's a boy. It's a boy. And a girl. It's a girl. Twins. It's a boy and a girl. We had twins, everyone. A boy and a girl." He rushed back into the room and closed the door.

It was Erica who said it, finally. "No wonder that poor woman was so big. She must be totally exhausted by now with two of them fighting their way out. We should leave and let her and Warren figure it out."

"Not a chance. We aren't leaving until their Uncle Jim gets to see the kids. Let's storm the barricades. Who's with me?"

Lily and James were first, but only because, like me, they didn't know any better. Maddie gave me an elbow. I called the dogs in and Zoe helped Zelda find the room. Max brought up the rear with me.

"Just a quick visit, you two. I couldn't keep the dogs

away. And the kids. I couldn't keep them away, either."

An exhausted Allie offered up the twins to Warren and he knelt down to let Lily and James see two little pink, fresh-faced babies for themselves.

"How will we ever tell them apart, James?" Lily wanted to know. "Look. They're identical."

Zelda snuffled and her cold, wet nose made its way from one lump to the other in Warren's arms, followed by Zoe and Max. Satisfied, Zelda nudged Zoe and she led her behind the waiting crowd. Erica and Hank and Maddie made their way into the room and wisely knew enough to not stay long.

"All right, people and dogs, let's go home. It's time for a cold one," I announced.

We piled into the Packard and I peeled back the top for the ride home. I knew by the grin pasted on James' face what was coming.

"Dad, could we ever get a car like this? It's so cool with the top down," he said.

"Well, one day, perhaps. Does it have to be as old as this one?"

"Oh no. It could be newer if that's what you want," James said.

Hank winked at me in the mirror. If James played his cards right, I thought his dad just might grant his wish.

I eased the Packard into the marina parking lot and the troupe gathered beneath the shade tree in front of the trailer.

"We'll bring up some of what we had for the reception before the action started," Maddie said. "Shamus, drag out the table. I'll get our umbrellas."

Hank and Erica went down the hill and returned with a wheelbarrow of ice and beer and food. I got out three bowls and put a little ice cream in them so the dogs could celebrate with us. "Watch this, everyone." I stood back and waited.

Zoe nudged Zelda. The dog followed her to her bowl. Zelda found it and snuffled her thanks. Zoe waited until Zelda's nose searched out the ice cream and she dug in. Satisfied, Zoe nudged Zelda and went to her own bowl. She worked it toward Zelda and side by side they lapped at their bits of ice cream.

"How long has Zelda been blind?" My voice quavered. It was all I could do to get the words out Lily and James put their arms around me. It was a small comfort.

"We didn't know how to tell you, Uncle Jim, so we thought we should let Zelda and Zoe tell you in their own way. We think it's about six months or so. We took Zelda to the vet as soon as we realized. There's nothing we can do. Zoe watches out for her," James said.

"I do too, Uncle Jim, like you asked. I promised, remember? James and me both promised."

"That's right. We watch over her together. Zoe worries over her, too. You saw that," James said.

"I remember, James. You too, Lily. Thank you both. It means so much to me that Zelda has good people loving her and taking care of her."

It was twilight when the celebration ended. Zoe left Zelda in my care and wandered down the hill with Max. Maddie and I sat out for a bit and then she went in. "I'll be in shortly. I want to sit with Zelda for a while longer."

I propped my back against the tree. Zelda lay at my side on her tummy, looking out across the water in the dying light. A bright full moon was rising. I wondered if she could see anything at all. I stroked her neck and ruffled her ears. Her cold nose found my hand and I enjoyed the sensation.

"You were a pretty girl in your fancy bandanna, Zelda.

Everyone commented on it." I stroked her neck and Zelda's tail swept the lawn. She sat up and nuzzled my face.

"Are you going to come in, Zelda? Your spot in the bedroom is waiting."

She looked at me in the dim light. It seemed as though she shook her head.

"I'll leave the door open for you. You can come in when you're ready."

She snuffled and settled in beside me. I waited a few more minutes before getting up. "I love you, Zelda. I miss you."

She woofed gently before resting her head on her forelegs.

"Good night, pretty girl. We'll see each other in the morning, okay?"

THIRTY-NINE

James and Lily bounded up the steps and ran headlong into the trailer without stopping. "How come the door is open, Uncle Jim?"

"I left it open for Zelda. She didn't want to come in when I did."

"Last night Zoe went up to get Zelda and she didn't come back. She's been with Zelda all night. I think there's something wrong with her."

"Go and see, Jim," Maddie said. "And put on some pants."

Zoe was indeed with Zelda. She must have remained by her side all night. She was nuzzling Zelda, trying to wake her up. I thought I knew why she hadn't been able to lead Zelda down the hill.

"James, take Lily and tell your dad to come up, would you? You'd better stay down there for now with Lily. Please?"

"All right. But what's wrong, Uncle Jim? Why didn't Zoe bring Zelda home?"

"Hank and I will figure it out, okay? Go down and send him up."

James called to Zoe but she wouldn't leave Zelda's side.

"Let Zoe stay with Zelda for now, James. She wants to

be with her friend."

I waited for Lily and James to go before I finished dressing.

"What's wrong? Is Zelda all right?" Maddie asked.

"I think Zelda left us last night, dear. I'm going out to check on her."

Zoe stopped nudging long enough to lick at my hand and then went back to work, nudging Zelda. I felt Zelda's nose. It was warm. I reached beneath her. I couldn't feel a heartbeat.

"She's gone, Zoe. Zelda is gone."

Hank joined me on the grass. I helped him roll Zelda on her side so he could better check for a heartbeat.

"I suspected this sooner or later," Hank said. "I'm sorry, Jim. I made arrangements with the vet to have her cremated when it happened. I hope you don't mind."

"I want to take her. Will you help me get her to the car? I want her up front with me. Will you tell Lily and James that I'm going with her. I know they love her so much, but—"

"I know. It's already arranged. I'll break it to them. The vet said it would be a day at most. Maybe by tonight, even—"

"I want to do that, too. I'll make a place for her, right where she sat every night. Would that be all right? Maybe James and Lily could help."

Hank nodded. He helped me carry Zelda to the Packard. Zoe trailed after us, worried and confused to see us carrying her friend. I put the top down and Hank called to a forlorn Zoe to accompany him down the hill.

The vet helped me bring Zelda in. I considered taking the bandana. She was so proud and happy when I tied it on. She knew it was special, just for her. I couldn't do it.

"Put her name tag in with her, please, if that's all right." The tag had been with Zelda since Lucy and the dog grooming shop.

"Leave the bandana on, too." It was important to me that Zelda wear both on her final journey.

The vet gave me directions to a funeral home. From there I went to an engraver and made sure to wait while he did what I wanted. When it was done, I was as content as I could be, given the circumstances. Come evening, in the cool of the day when Zelda liked to relax on the grass, I would prepare a place for her.

I found the wheelbarrow and collected rocks and picked some wild flowers I saw Zelda sniffing when she came up the hill. Lily and James helped. Nobody talked much. We unloaded the rocks and watered the flowers. Everything was ready.

"Thank you for helping me, James and Lily. I couldn't have done it without your help."

The kids left to go to bed. Hank and Erica would bring them when it was time.

I was a wreck. Maddie and Friday kept me going. I told her about the fight in the parking lot with the feds after I threatened them.

"I wondered if it was something like that," she said. She seemed relieved to hear it.

"Allie and Warren have twins. You're taking care of Zelda. It's all good," she assured me.

"Yes, it is. Full circle." I didn't tell her why. Maybe one day. I only knew Zelda died of a broken heart, and it was my fault.

It was always my fault.

FORTY

The day broke cool and sunny. I took everyone for ice cream before ending up at the hospital. We learned our new mom had been released with her twin bundles of joy. We must have passed them on the way, but we missed them in the rush with everyone wanting me to drive faster to see the newborns.

"Do they have names yet? Does anyone know? How come Allie and Uncle Warren didn't call us, mom? We need to know these things."

A patient Erica smiled. "We'll know when they want to tell us, dear. It's our duty to wait and learn."

I made a quick stop at the mall. I didn't tell anyone why. I ran in and out in record time to get us back to the marina, where I took a call from the vet.

Zelda's remains were ready. I told Hank, and he went to talk to Erica. She allowed James and Lily to come with me. They brought Zoe and Friday. I took Maddie for moral support.

I asked them all to wait in the car. It would be a better wait than entering the clinic with the antiseptic smells and the other animals. When I came out, everyone was waiting to see Zelda.

"It's gorgeous, Jim."

Zelda's container was a deep, rich bronze. I made sure to show everyone Zelda's name engraved in a flourishing script. Underneath it said *The best dog ever.* Lily and James each took a turn holding her on the drive home.

"I picked up another bandana for her. I left the other one with her. And her tag, too. She had that same name tag from when I first met her with, with—" I couldn't go on.

"She's so light, Uncle Jim," Lily said.

"That's because Zelda is looking down on all of us. She knows already how much we miss her. How much we're going to miss her."

I didn't know what else to say.

Just before sundown, the entire crew made their way up the hill to the tree. Lily and James helped me lower Zelda. The bandana fit over the bronze container perfectly. Zelda would be so proud. I covered her and Lily and James brought a beach sunflower to plant with the wild flowers. I made sure to surround her bed with small rocks.

"Zelda wouldn't like it if someone stepped on her tail when she wasn't looking," I tried to explain. It was all I could do.

"We'll look after her, Uncle Jim. James and me. We'll take care of Zelda for you when you aren't here," Lily said.

"I know you will. Thank you. Knowing that means a lot to me. And to Zelda." I hugged them and thanked them and I could barely do that.

Allie and Warren cheered us up by sharing some news. The twins had names—Lisa after Allie's mother, and Logan after Warren's father.

It was a fitting end to a very long day for everyone.

FORTY-ONE

Maddie and I stayed another couple of days. We enjoyed spending the time just hanging out with everyone. I kept Zelda's flowers watered first thing in the morning. James and Lily and Zoe did the same in the cool of the evening.

I filled Hank and Warren in on what I discussed with their black-suited friends in the mall. I didn't tell them I promised to blow the entire operation sky-high if they ever set foot on marina property again. They were grateful. Allie wouldn't know. That made all three of us happy, Maddie included to make four.

Finally, it was time. We packed and loaded the Packard. Maddie drew Lily aside. I couldn't hear what was said, but the parting was teary for both of them.

"Mom took us to the mall. We found bandanas just like Zelda's, Uncle Jim. We got matching ones for Max and Zoe to have."

Lily tied it around her Max along with a collar and a name tag. It said *Max Friday*. Our business address and both phone numbers were engraved beneath. Maddie wasn't sure what to think.

"I called him Max Friday because Max is his very first name, and Friday is his last name when you found him,

Maddie," Lily explained. "Just like a person. And James said we should put both our phone numbers on the name tag, just in case."

Maddie bawled her eyes out a second time. I wasn't that far from it myself when I saw Zoe looking proud and happy in her own matching bandana.

"We decided to let Max go with Aunt Maddie, Uncle Jim. I talked it over with James. He says it's okay, right James?"

James nodded and took over. "We're both getting busy with school sports. We want to play soccer and baseball and do other stuff."

"That's right. Taking care of two dogs is really hard," Lily added.

"Yes, especially having to exercise them and everything."

Max looked from the kids to Maddie and back. I think he was deciding on his own if he was going to stay or go. Eventually, he sat down beside Maddie. The kids gave him a last hug.

"Zoe is going to miss Zelda. They were good company for each other," I said.

"Me and James already talked about that, Uncle Jim. We'll help Zoe get along, just like she helped Zelda."

That was all I needed. Maddie too. I opened the Packard's door, and Friday jumped into the back without invitation.

FORTY-TWO

Warren and Allie wheeled the newborns up the hill to see us off. They allowed Friday a final sniff of fresh baby scent and then Allie eased into a chair to watch the proceedings. Zoe came to say goodbye, too.

We hugged too many times and said teary goodbyes. Everyone followed us to the Packard. James called out. "Are you going to put the top down, Uncle Jim?"

The huge grin said he was pleased when I did. The last thing I heard was James asking his dad if they could get a convertible one day. I wondered how long it would take Hank to break down. He treated James like he was his own, and Lily too, of course.

It was a long, slow drive to the highway, where I kept it under the limit, knowing I would be passing through crazytown. We were a couple of miles past the town when the blues flashing in the mirror drew Allie's attention.

"Oh no. Not again. Jim—"

"I see them. We're almost there." I stepped on the gas and the reliable old Packard's engine kicked in and did its duty. The distance between the cars increased. "It looks like they didn't get the memo."

"Are you ever going to tell me?"

"Absolutely. But right now, I have something else that

needs doing." The gas pedal halted at the floor. "When we hit the county line, you won't be able to shut me up."

I called back to Friday. "Hang on, dog. It might get a little breezy back there."

Friday's bandana flapped in the wind. We made the county line with miles to spare. The cruiser was nowhere in sight. Maddie settled back in her seat and opened a well-worn book.

"What's it called?" Allie held it up. "It's written by someone called Dr. Spock. I'm just getting to the part where he talks about water breaking. Shall I read it to you?"

Friday's cold nose hit the back of my neck, mimicking Zelda's trick, but I was ahead of him. I already knew not to utter a single word.

It was time to move on. Zelda's passing had lifted a great weight from my shoulders. I allowed Zelda to take all my regrets away with her. I was able to let Lucy and Kara and Pilar go with her. It was time to stop living with too many memories from my past.

It was time to get on with life and build new memories.

BREAKDOWN

PX DUKE

1

I helped my partner, Maddie Spence, downstairs with her bags. It seemed like there were a lot of them, but maybe I was worrying too much. After all, she was leaving Friday with me. That by itself was unusual, considering she and the dog were inseparable. Each had adopted the other when he jumped into her car at a rest stop.

"You're coming back, right?" I asked.

Of course she was. Friday looked from Maddie to me and back. His tail wasn't wagging. I suspect he, too, was concerned when he saw the suitcases.

"Friday wouldn't like to find out you left him all alone with no explanation," I added for effect.

The dog was sitting by the passenger door to Maddie's little yellow compact. He kept looking from his mistress to me and the car.

"See? He's concerned there's something you aren't telling him."

Maddie rolled her eyes. "Do you think there's something I'm not telling you, Detective Nash?"

"Well—" I got down on one knee to pet Friday. "I'm pretty sure you're not abandoning Friday. Lily would hunt you down."

Friday's ears perked up when he heard the girl's name and he snorted.

"What else are you pretty sure of?" Maddie asked.

If she was leaving Friday with me, it had to mean she was coming back. Heck, we hadn't even had a fight yet. Or had we? I thought for a moment but couldn't remember. "If you aren't coming back, does that mean I get the dog? To keep?"

"Nah. I'll send for him. Right, Friday?"

Mollified, Friday barked. I couldn't tell if he knew all about it, or if he was making it up as he went along.

I finished loading the bags into the tiny car's trunk. "You sure are taking a lot of luggage. How long are you planning on staying?"

I leaned with both hands and the trunk snapped shut. I think Friday sensed my concern. His head was still busy, moving from one of us to the other.

Maddie reached to pet her dog. "Friday."

He looked up at her. His head tilted. His ears perked. His tail stilled. I was pretty sure he was waiting for his mistress to open the door.

"Stay with Jim. Okay?" she said to the dog.

The dog went sad-sack all of a sudden, finally knowing for sure he wouldn't be going on this car ride. His entire body seemed to collapse. His tail sagged. He looked at me with sad-sack brown eyes and a forlorn expression on his furry face.

"You do what Jim tells you," she added.

Friday's head drooped even lower, if that was possible. I think mine did, too, now that the goodbyes were over. We were a pair, not wanting Maddie to leave. Both of us wanted to go with her for moral support. Or something.

"Jim, take care of my dog."

Was there any doubt?

"Friday. Take care of Jim."

I don't think Friday was so sure. Maddie brought out

the bandana Lily bestowed on Friday and tied it around his neck. That seemed to cheer him up. Me too, come to think of it.

"What a handsome boy you are," she told him.

That did it for Friday. He was happy. Already I knew he'd be prancing up the stairs like he was the best boy ever. Which he was.

"As for you, sailor—" she began.

"Am I going to get a bandana, too?".

"No. You're going to get something even better," she insisted.

Maddie wrapped her arms around me and kissed me like she was already away for a week. "That ought to hold you."

Friday barked, but he was probably jealous. We stayed downstairs until the car disappeared from sight.

"All right, dog." I opened the door and waited. "I'm the boss now."

The dog didn't seem to think so. Friday couldn't be bothered to even give me a look before prancing past and heading up the stairs.

2

Sandy Franklin picked up his daughter and placed her in her high chair at the table. He found a clean bib and tied it around her neck through a scramble of arms and hands. Holly, his daughter, struggled to turn in the chair, impatient, wanting to see what was going on with the stove.

"It's ready, dear," he told her.

Holly wasn't convinced. She screwed up her face around the soother and looked at her father. He attached the tray to the high chair through waving arms. When it was done, Holly's tiny hands slapped at it, anxious to see her food coming.

"I wouldn't lie to you," he said

Holly's eyes grew big following the waffle floating in front of her father from over the stove to the plate on the high chair table. She grinned past the soother stuck in her mouth and spit it out. It flew past the tray and bounced on the floor, where it disappeared.

Sandy spread a dab of butter and a teeny tiny bit of syrup on the warm waffle. "Careful, dear. Hot."

Holly dabbed at the waffle cautiously with a finger. A hole appeared before she finally picked the waffle up whole. Using both hands, she raised it to her mouth and taste-tested. A huge smile appeared. Her feet kicked. Her mouth broke with the smile and began chewing.

"Mmm. Is that good or what?" her father asked.

She mimicked her father's *Mmm* as best she could with a full mouth while still managing to chew.

With Holly quieted until the waffle disappeared, Sandy looked around the kitchen. Waffle mix and a pot and utensils cluttered the counter. Milk and orange juice and apple juice and syrup and whatever Holly might want next was scattered on the table. He didn't like to feed her the sweets, but sometimes it was the only thing that would soothe her. He liked Angela, his wife and Holly's mom, to come and go in peace. She wasn't a fan of feeding sweets to Holly.

Angela—Angie—was the bread-winner of the family. They discussed it endlessly before the baby was born. She had the better job. It paid double his salary. Thus he—both of them, actually—agreed he would stay home and take care of their first child.

Sandy grew comfortable with it over the almost two years. He was thoroughly enjoying it but for the sleepless nights and long days. Even so, he managed to convince himself it wasn't so bad. The dark circles beneath his eyes were his reward for allowing his wife to provide for the three of them.

He told himself he didn't mind again and again. Perhaps there was just a bit of repressed resentment every day when his wife left the harried household behind, looking fit and trim and dressed to the nines. Her job as a corporate financial adviser demanded it. She worked with the really high-priced help. Her work helped the brass make the choices that got them their fancy cars and big bonuses.

He didn't begrudge her that, although he knew she wasn't exactly enamored of doing all the work for someone else to take home the lottery. That was what her job entailed, though, and Angela was accustomed to it.

It seemed like it rankled her less and less.

3

ngela Franklin's morning wasn't off to a great start. She went to bed late. Working on her presentation long past her usual bedtime kept her up. The coffee didn't help, either. Sandy admonished her every time he got up to soothe restless Holly. To satisfy him, she reluctantly ended up bringing the laptop into their bed. Exhausted when she finally went to sleep, she didn't wake up until twenty minutes past her alarm.

She checked her lifeblood. The laptop on the bed beside her was dead. She had neglected to plug it in when she finally went to sleep. There was no hope for it. She discarded it in her bag and checked her phone. It too was on its last legs. She would have to charge the phone in the car.

She remembered the USB dongle attached to her laptop. She plucked at the tiny plug and dropped it into a pocket in her purse. It contained the only copy of her project and the extensive profiles of the three companies being considered for buyouts. With any luck, it would be the last work she did on them. The entire project was becoming boring. She wanted something new to sink her teeth into. This morning's meeting would tell the tale.

She showered and dried her hair and did makeup and

checked her reflection in the bedroom mirror. Satisfied, she headed downstairs, clutching her work bag and her purse with both hands. She halted in the doorway to the kitchen and watched Sandy happily feeding a cooing Holly. Her daughter was digging into the waffle like it was the last one she would ever see.

She surveyed the bombed-out kitchen. The normally neat and tidy island was a breakfast mess, thanks to Sandy. Waffle-making goods, cups, saucers, cutlery, milk, lay scattered everywhere. She spotted the juice containers.

"I thought we agreed no sweet juice first thing in the morning," she reminded him.

Sandy turned to face her and immediately she regretted saying it. It was obvious her husband hadn't slept well, as evidenced by the dark circles around his eyes.

"I know, dear, but sometimes agreements are made to be broken. You must know that from work."

Was it a dig at her job? She wasn't sure. Was he trying to make one on purpose? He had to be too tired for that.

"You look nice this morning," Sandy told her.

She sighted loudly. "No I don't. I'm a mess. I stayed up too late."

He was about to admonish her, but instead swallowed hard enough for her to hear. He called to her several times throughout the night. She ignored him every time. He didn't know she was in bed until he woke to find her getting in beside him. That was when he noticed the laptop on the bed.

"Big day today?" he asked.

She rarely kept her husband advised about what she was working on. He only knew she liked her job, for the most part. They both liked the paydays, even if her hours were too long and the days too short. He didn't hold it against her. She always made time for their daughter, no matter how exhausted she was when she got home.

Lately, that bedtime was becoming later and later.

Rarely did she make it before Holly was in bed. Usually by then he was grabbing a few hours of peace and quiet under a blanket on the sofa. Sometimes she would leave him sleeping while she went upstairs to her office to continue working.

She knew that always annoyed him, but she knew he swallowed his pride, too. It was all about the payday and the future for the three of them. He was constantly telling her she would be rewarded for her diligence and work ethic.

She wasn't so certain, and she made it plain to him. Her last raise was a year ago. This year's expected Christmas bonus didn't happen. The powers that be made the announcement at the party. No bonuses for last year. Try harder for the next.

So she tried harder, and she was convinced she would make it this year.

"Don't forget I'm taking the car in for a service today," Sandy told her.

She cursed silently, knowing she would be forced to drive the truck. "You need to get rid of that truck. It's dangerous. The brakes. The transmission. You said you were going to put lap belts in it and you haven't."

It occurred to her she shouldn't have said any of it. After all, the truck was his baby. He had it before they were married. His dream was to finish it properly, seat belts and all. Even she knew it would be one sweet ride when it was done. If it ever got done.

"I know, dear. I just don't have the energy any more. Holly is taking up all of it. The park. Walks. The stroller. Meals. Play time. My time is Holly time."

Immediately, she regretted admonishing him. She was the worker bee. It was Sandy's job to support her by dedicating his time to care for their daughter. Still, on weekends, when it was Angela's turn to spend time with Holly, she called her *Mommy*. She was still calling her father *Dada*, and he spent five non-stop days a week with her. So far, there was no calling her father *Daddy* in Holly's little world.

She heard the sigh, and knew exactly what he was thinking. There was no justice.

4

Angela kissed her husband and daughter goodbye before making for the truck and then remembered the keys. Sandy grinned, already waiting at the door to switch them out. Holly waved furiously, calling out Goodbye mommy again and again. It was their standard ritual. Angela kissed her daughter a last time on the way to the half-ton.

She stepped outside into the sunshine and hesitated. The day was starting auspiciously. A bright blue sky would take her to work. A light breeze whispered through the leaves of a nearby tree on their lot. The truck was parked beneath it. It was a real antique, even if it wasn't classified as one. Antique was too kind a word for it.

While her husband perfected the exterior before they were married, he couldn't find the time or the inclination to work on it since. The interior was beat. A blanket covered the ragged seat. The huge steering wheel was no longer round. The automatic transmission clunked into every gear. She looked out over a faded and cracked dash. He never even bothered to get one of those cheap auto-store covers for it.

She turned the key and a cloud of blue smoke engulfed the driveway, drifting off in the breeze. She wondered if the neighbors would complain again as she wrestled to get the shift lever into reverse. It caught and she jerked into the street. She made another try to find drive and she was off.

She barely heard Holly's repeated goodbyes over the exhaust sound. She waved a final time before disappearing around a corner. Her grip on the wheel relaxed and then tightened again when she remembered the presentation she was scheduled to do.

She fished for her phone and the charging cable in her purse. Went to plug it in before catching herself. There was no outlet. Instead, a cigarette lighter filled the spot on the dash. How many times had she asked for it to be replaced with an adapter so she could plug in her phone? She lost count. She cursed silently and tossed the dead phone on the seat.

That and a dead laptop. What else could go wrong? She reached across for her purse. The truck swerved. She fought with the steering to get it back in her lane. Carefully now, she checked the pocket in her purse.

The feel of the USB dongle reassured her that at least it was still there, and she was smug in the knowledge that her presentation would be a go. She would borrow a laptop. Satisfied, she concentrated on maneuvering the truck through traffic.

She fought with the ancient power steering. She struggled with the old brakes. Sandy explained the truck's eccentricities to her many times, but it was like her first time at the wheel. Resigned to being late, she concentrated on rehearsing the presentation she would be giving.

The black SUV on her tail was following too close. She kept looking in the mirror, wondering if she should brake-check the driver to wake him up.

She turned off the busy main street. As she did, she checked the mirror. The SUV was still there. Obviously they both wanted to make time by taking a less busy shortcut. She had done it many times. She halted at a stop sign, looked both ways, and was immediately blocked by a vehicle cutting in front of her.

She cursed and wrestled with the shift lever in an effort to back up and go around. The transmission locked. The truck would move neither forward nor back. The truck's door flew open. A hand grabbed her hair and hauled her out. She fell on her knees. Someone climbed over her to grab her laptop bag.

Two men forced a black hood over her head. They secured her wrists before manhandling her into the vehicle. Doors slammed and the SUV accelerated away.

She rocked from side to side as the SUV made a series of rapid turns before the driver gunned the accelerator. They had to be on a straightaway to make good time.

Angela's first panicked thoughts were about her project presentation. There was no one to replace her. Her concerns came to an abrupt halt when she finally realized that was the least of her problems. Immediately her thoughts turned to Holly and Sandy.

She was in trouble. Big trouble. And she had no idea why.

5

Sandy surveyed the clean kitchen. He had a routine, a system, and it never took him long to neat it up. He busied himself readying the three-wheeled stroller for his daily run. Water for him and for Holly. Sunscreen for the park if they stopped today. Never his phone, though. His morning run was his me time. He and Holly.

He tucked a sweet juice into the stroller. It was a reward they would share. "Don't tell mommy, okay Holly?"

She looked up at him and giggled. "No-no, Dada." Holly didn't mind in the slightest.

"We'll be sure to brush our teeth after."

He loaded Holly into the stroller. She was always happy to know they were going somewhere. She cooed and giggled and laughed and waved at strangers as they went speeding down the sidewalks on their run with the three-wheeled stroller. The stop at the park lasted only long enough for a brief swing and to share the juice. By the time they returned, Holly was as fatigued as he was with all of her arm-waving and smiling and calling out to strangers.

Sandy gave Holly her bathroom break before changing her outfit and putting her to bed for her nap. Her eyes closed the instant she went down. In sympathy, as he liked to call it, he stretched out on the sofa and closed his eyes. He went off to dreamland as quickly as Holly. He kept one ear tuned, in case she should wake before he did.

He woke with a start and checked the time. He almost slept past the service appointment for their fancy car. He woke Holly. She opened her eyes and grinned up at him. "Are you ready for a car ride, Holly?"

She reached out her arms and he picked her up and put her in her high chair. "How about a snack before we go?"

She nodded and called out *Cerweal pwease* in her little-girl voice.

"Cereal it is. I think I'll join you."

He filled two bowls, but Holly wasn't having it. She reached for his, wanting to eat out of it. He obliged her with a single spoon for both of them.

"All right. It's time. Do you need to go to the bathroom?"

She nodded and he took her, waiting until she finished. "Good girl, dear. Now, where did I put that soother?"

At the sound of the word, Holly perked up instantly. Her eyes grew large. Her head turned from side to side, searching, looking around. She couldn't see it, either. She was on the verge of tears when Sandy popped it into her mouth. Her eyes closed and she grinned past it, showing tiny white teeth in the process.

He carried her to the SUV and strapped her in the back. He slipped one of her shoes off and placed it in his lap. It was a little trick someone told him about. It made sure he never forgot she was back there. Sure enough, even after her nap, she quieted and was dozing off by the time he turned into the dealership. A car ride always did that for her.

"All right, dear. We're here."

He picked the soother up from the back seat and

popped it into her mouth while he replaced her shoe. He dropped the keys off and he carried her part-way to a park bench. He put her down to let her walk the rest of the way on her short, sturdy little legs. At the bench, she held out her arms and he lifted her up to sit beside him. Together, they amused themselves by watching people and dogs strolling by.

"Puppy, Dada. Puppy."

Holly pointed and giggled and kicked her feet. He was tempted to put her down so she could investigate on her own. In the end he thought better of it. He didn't know the owner, and he'd be darned if he'd let a strange, unknown dog near his daughter.

He went for his back pocket to check the time and discovered he'd forgotten his phone. He cursed his forgetfulness silently and picked Holly up. They traded the bench for the swing.

It took only three pushes for Holly to begin laughing and squealing with delight. "Push, Dada, push."

Sandy pushed. Holly laughed and giggled. Finally, it was time to return to the dealer. He picked up a pink-faced, happy Holly. "Let's go see how they're doing with our car."

"Car wide, Dada? Car wide?"

He drove home, gave Holly a bathroom break, and prepared a late lunch for two. Following that, he took her out for a swing in the back yard before putting her down. As was his wont, he stretched out on the sofa and crashed.

6

Groggy and still half asleep, Sandy tuned an ear. It wasn't Holly. He listened again. It was his darned phone, the phone he forgot to take with him. He'd only turned it on its face, forgetting to turn it off. He checked the time, revealing the unfamiliar number. One-thirty. He was out longer than he thought.

He cocked an ear to listen for Holly, but she was still sleeping. He didn't like her to be down for too long. It meant when she went to bed, she wouldn't sleep until late into the evening.

"Hello?" He was groggy and confused from his nap. He probably shouldn't have answered.

"Is this Sandy Franklin?"

"Yes."

Now he was intrigued. He quickly ran through a list in his head. All the bills, paid. That was the extent of it. It was his job to never leave anything unpaid. He saw to it assiduously. Perhaps it was the car dealership.

"Who's calling, please?"

The garage where he took the car? He paid by credit card. It couldn't be that. He hadn't left Holly behind. She was upstairs, sleeping. To be certain, he climbed the stairs to look in on Holly in her crib.

"Hello?"

Mumbling came through the phone. Other voices in the background.

"Hello. Who's there?"

"Sandy?"

"Yes. Who is this?"

"It's Bill Henry from Angela's office."

"Oh. Hello. Yes." His wife's boss. "What can I do for you?"

"It's about Angela. She didn't come in today. Do you know where she is?"

He recalled the presentation his wife told him about. She was scheduled to give it this morning. It was important, according to her. She wouldn't slough it off. Wasn't it supposed to go first thing? Why was her boss only calling now?

"Hang on."

Sandy scrolled through numerous text messages and several voice mails from the same number. So they had called earlier. He missed them all when he forgot to take the phone with him to the garage.

"Angela isn't here. Did you try her cell?" Sandy asked.

"Yes. More than once. She's not picking up. We texted, too. She was scheduled to give a presentation this morning. It's long overdue now. We've given up and postponed everything. Do you think you could track her down?"

It was the truck. It had to be. She hated driving it. Maybe the brakes failed. Or the steering. She was in a hospital somewhere. Damn but he should have put seat belts in it. She was always asking when he'd get around to it. Every time he put her off.

"I'll make some calls and get back to you, all right?" Sandy said.

Sandy hung up immediately. Considered waking Holly so she wouldn't stay up late. Thought better of it and called Angie's cell phone instead. The call went straight to voice mail.

All right, he remembered her phone was dead when she left. The adapter. He meant to pick one up to wire the truck's lighter. She wouldn't be able to charge her phone or make any calls. But it was after lunch. She should have been at work long ago. He checked the first text asking about the whereabouts of his wife.

Nine o'clock. She would have been a half-hour late by then.

What to do. What to do.

Sandy paced the living room and tried thinking things through. Police. Would they know anything? Perhaps about an accident. But didn't they only look into missing people after two or three days? It was hardly that. He would call anyway.

Sandy hung up the phone, disappointed, worried, and no further ahead. There were no accidents involving his truck. The desk officer was nice enough to check with the 911 operations center. There were no calls reporting the plate number for anything amiss. He debated calling the hospitals, but thought better of it. If the 911 center had no records—

As far as the missing person report, it was just as he suspected—too soon.

7

There it was again, filtering up from the ground floor. I tuned an ear to the door and listened ever more closely. The cries were getting louder. Friday's ears perked up. He was on alert, too. His tail halted its wagging. He positioned to face the door. His head tilted and a confused expression appeared on his furry black face. I recognized the sound, finally, and admonished the dog.

"You can relax, Friday. I don't think they'll be coming in here. They're looking for someone else."

The dog took my advice and returned to his bed between the office desks. In seconds he took up the position he was in before the commotion began.

"You're getting far too much sleep, Friday. Maddie wouldn't be happy knowing we didn't go for our walk yet." I held a finger to my lips, something I learned from Lily. "*Shh.* If you don't tell, I certainly won't. It's all okay."

The commotion started all over again, and then it appeared to hesitate on the second floor landing. Slow steps halted at the closed door. A knock sounded, tentative and barely audible.

Okay, so maybe Friday was right after all. I called

through the closed door. "You can come in. It's open."

A tall man in a rumpled shirt pushed the door open. Dark-rimmed eyes wandered the office and then paused to look me over. A colorful blanket covered an indiscriminate lump hanging over the man's left shoulder. I heard snuffling. I recognized it because it was what Friday did sometimes. Not quite, but it was close.

The man offloaded the lump of blanket from his shoulder into both hands and turned it around. A pink-faced baby peeked out past the blanket and examined me with bright blue eyes. Okay, so not exactly a baby. A baby perhaps two years old. Maybe younger. I was no expert in that department. I suddenly remembered an expression—*the terrible twos*.

The man eased the blanket back to reveal tangled, curly red hair poking up. A pink hoodie matched the girl's teary pink face. Pink pants completed the outfit. The baby's outfit. The man was dressed normally but for the badly wrinkled shirt.

"I take it this is the private detective's office. Are you Jim Nash?"

"That I am. And you are—?" I waited.

"Franklin. Sandy Franklin. This is our daughter, Holly."

At the mention of her name, Holly spit out the soother that was formerly firmly clenched between her teeth. It arced, hit the floor, and bounced out of sight. High-pitched screams filled the office the instant it left the confines of the little girl's mouth. Piercing screams.

Holly's head circled, first left, then right, searching, before tilting up at her father. It was obvious even to me she wanted to follow the soother to the floor. Kicking feet and waving arms told me Holly was probably a handful. I didn't need to be a detective to figure that out.

"Pleased to meet you, Sandy. Hello, Holly."

Holly's blue eyes focused on me. It was probably the strange voice. Her screaming halted and she forgot all about the missing soother. She seemed to look me over and then, as though suddenly remembering she was absent something, began screaming all over again.

I wasn't surprised. I was known to affect some women that way.

Sandy sat his daughter on the floor. She worked herself onto hands and knees and began investigating her new surroundings.

A very wise Friday stayed put between the desks. I think he even tried making himself smaller by pulling back against the wall. He may have been trying to process exactly what was happening in his normally much quieter domain.

Holly's blue eyes locked onto the dog. Before Friday could affect a nervous blink, she screamed. "Puppy!"

Friday wheezed and sat up and looked over at me. I remained nonchalant, trying to appear as though everything going on in our lives in this instant was the most normal thing ever.

The little girl pushed herself back onto her feet. She swayed back and forth. She swung her arms to help steady herself. She waddled her way toward Friday on short, sturdy legs and white-laced pink sneakers covering feet attached to the end of them. She wavered with every tentative step. Changed direction at least once on the way before correcting herself. It looked as though she might fall down any second.

She got within what she must have considered hailing distance. She held out her short little arms straight ahead and splayed fingers and cooed.

Friday looked up at me again. I thought for sure he was about to put tail between legs and slink off before anyone noticed, especially his short little new best friend.

"You're too late, Friday. Holly is on her way to introducing herself."

The soother was forgotten. Holly slipped and landed on her well-padded rear. She leaned forward on hands and knees and made a feeble attempt to push herself up.

Duly intrigued, Friday reluctantly got up on all fours.

Holly's head looked up at the dog and she immediately ended up splayed out on the floor a second time.

"Puppy. Nice puppy," she exclaimed.

Resigned to the little girl's distress, Friday stood over her. He gripped the back of the hoodie in his teeth and lifted the girl up. He set her down on her feet and released her. Holly giggled and promptly sat down. Friday picked her up again and this time she stayed up. Her stubby little arms circled Friday's neck and she cooed into his ear.

"Puppy."

Satisfied the girl wouldn't be falling down until she released him, Friday sat back on his haunches and kept a wary eye on Holly. Her arms remained locked around his neck. I looked over at Sandy. He was grinning like a proud father. Come to think of it, so was I.

"Furry." Holly wasn't about to be silenced by her discovery. "Puppy furry." Holly buried her face in Friday's neck. Her grip slipped and she ended up on her rear.

Friday sighed a doggie sigh and looked up at me.

"You're on your own, dog."

Holly wasn't so sure. She called to the dog. "Ups. Ups. Puppy. Ups."

Resigned to the possibility that he might end up being Holly's helper for the rest of his life, Friday did as requested.

The little girl giggled and, back on two sturdy, upright legs, wrapped her arms around Friday's furry neck once more and giggled.

"Now that Holly seems to have Friday under control, what can I do for you, Mr. Franklin?"

"I think my wife, Angela—Holly's mother—has gone missing."

Sandy Franklin was a remarkably patient man to sit through all that before declaring a missing wife.

8

Sandy Franklin knew the dog wouldn't hold Holly's attention forever. Without a word he got down on his hands and knees. The man craned his neck as he searched high and low for his daughter's missing soother. He found it and looked furtively at her holding onto the dog's neck. He wiped the soother on a pant leg and jammed it into a pocket before standing up.

"We're trying to wean her off of it," he explained.

"How's that working for you?"

"Not well, but we keep trying," he repeated.

"So why did you find my office again, Mr. Franklin?"

I looked at my phone. Three p.m. I turned it over and placed it face down on the desk.

"It's my wife. Holly's mother, Angela. She seems to be missing."

I opened a drawer and took out a notebook. "What leads you to that conclusion?" I noted the date and time and the man's name and that of his wife and daughter. His eyes traveled to the little girl with her arms wrapped firmly around an uncomplaining Friday and then up at me.

"We had our normal breakfast. As you can imagine, it was rushed with Holly refusing to eat and crying and banging things and scattering food. I like to get Holly to the table early so Angie can get dressed in peace and quiet. She works. I'm a stay-at-home dad."

I wanted to get things back on track. "You were saying she was missing."

"Oh, yes, well, we were arguing about what time she'd be home. We had a dinner date with some neighbors. A barbecue. Sometimes she gets back late, and I wanted to be sure she'd be home in time."

He looked down at Holly.

"Anyway, she leaves around seven-thirty every morning. Drives herself to work for eight-thirty. By nine the office was calling wondering where she was. Apparently she was supposed to be at an important meeting first thing and never showed. No phone call, nothing."

I scratched more notes before looking up. "Who does your wife work for?"

He told me. It was a venture capital firm. In a previous life I worked part-time for one of the biggest. "I've heard of them."

The company bought up near-bankrupt outfits, sold off assets that were worth anything, and let the remainder die. It laid off or fired employees left, right and center in the process to reduce costs. Pension and retirement benefits, everything, went out the window. Sandy interrupted my thoughts.

"They buy up solvent companies, too. Not many, but a few."

"Her job has to be high-pressure. Do you know if she has any enemies?" I asked.

He thought before replying. "Not that I know of. Although I guess anything is possible given the nature of her work."

"And that is?"

"She runs the numbers on the companies before the

firm buys them. If the numbers aren't good, they don't buy."

"So she does financial audits and investigations. Maybe saves some companies, lets others collapse in bankruptcy."

"I suppose that's one way of putting it," Sandy said.

I scribbled more notes. "It's possible she might not have made many friends in the companies she allowed to go bust."

"That's possible, yes."

Holly was suddenly quiet. I looked over at Friday. He was stretched out on his bed. Holly was snuggled against him with her face buried in his neck. She was breathing quietly, fast asleep. The one eye Friday was trying to keep on the little girl appeared to look relieved.

I turned back to Sandy Franklin. "You mentioned something about an important meeting that required your wife's presence this morning. Do you know what it was about? Perhaps a takeover? Maybe the outfit's owners weren't happy with her decision."

Sandy considered. "It could be something like that, yes. My first thought was to go to the police."

So he hadn't gone that route. "Why didn't you?"

"I didn't think a few hours was enough for them to do anything," he said. "Was I right?"

He was. I didn't say so. I asked what kind of car she drove. The plate number.

"I did call to ask about accidents," he added.

He called the police after all. Probably smart of him to ask. "Is it possible the car broke down?"

He considered. "I suppose. But we have a road service. It wouldn't take her this long to get to work even if it did. No. Wait. That's not right. Her phone was dead. And she couldn't use it in the truck. I never installed an adapter."

The truck she drove to work was old. I continued making notes, halting when Sandy's phone rang.

"It's her." He held the phone to show me.

"Honey. Where are you? Work has been calling all morning. I'm at a—"

Sandy halted, listening. "I'm going to put you on speaker, okay? I'm doing laundry."

Chalk one up for Sandy. His wife's voice was shaky. Trembling. Trying to remain calm and not doing a good job of it. The woman's breathing came in spurts between sentences.

Angela Franklin was barely keeping it together.

9

Demands. **Surely the** kidnappers would have demands. The demands would come after the How are you-I'm fine tear-filled and panicked talk between husband and wife. The phone would be surrendered and the kidnappers would talk. But when it was over, they didn't have demands. They hung up. Perhaps it was more of a getting-to-know-you phone call. I was confused, to say the least.

So was Sandy. I asked the obvious question. "Did you recognize anything? Any familiar sounds in the background?" I couldn't ask if he recognized any kidnapper voices. None of them talked.

"No. I'm just relieved she's okay. She's okay." He looked down at his daughter nestled against Friday and smiled.

"What did you do before you quit work to take care of Holly, Mr. Franklin?"

"I was a computer programmer. I worked on the shady side of things. Testing. Probing. Looking for weaknesses in systems. That kind of thing."

"Ever do any hacking?"

He looked at me, as though sizing me up. "Well—"

I waited.

"Yes. Plenty. I was good at it, too."

There it was. I had a glimmer. "You've been away from the business for two years or so. Do any of your old friends miss you?"

"Oh yeah. Some. Mostly the second-rate ones. I carried a lot of their weight."

I considered a moment before asking. "Perhaps one of your old friends has been hired to break into your wife's computer to obtain inside information. Is that possible?"

"She does sensitive work. Collects a lot of data and parses it for the higher ups. What she presents determines whether the company she researches will be a buy or an ignore or a sell. Whether it will be parted out and sold bit by bit. Destroyed and dumped once the value is gone. That kind of thing."

I think I got it. I made more notes before putting down the pencil. "All right, Mr. Franklin. I'll look for your wife. I'm going to call a friend of mine at the local PD. You don't need to know who he is."

Sandy Franklin reached into his bag and pulled out a checkbook. He filled it out without asking what my services were going to cost. He handed it over, and as much as I didn't want to look, I did anyway.

"Fill in any amount you want, Mr. Nash. Anything at all. Holly needs her mother, even though right now it seems she needs Friday, too."

He bent to pick up his little girl. She opened drowsy eyes and grinned at him. Turned her head to look at me. I grinned right back. Friday, ever the watchful dog with the children, sat up and snorted.

"Bye puppy."

"His name is Friday, dear."

"Bye *Fwiday*. Bye."

Short pink fingers attached to a pink hand with an arm covered by a pink sleeve waved at the dog from her father's arms.

"Bye Fwiday. Bye Fwiday."

Friday woofed and followed them to the stairs. Holly called out all the way down to the door. Friday woofed his own goodbyes every time she called his name until the door closed on the pair and they were in the street.

"Well, Fwiday." The dog tilted his head and looked up at me like I should have known he was only being nice for the little girl's sake.

"It looks like we have a new client. Come on. We're going for a car ride."

That was all it took to get the dog taking the lead down the stairs. He halted at the car and I opened the door. "You didn't even call shotgun, dog. Did meeting your new bestie make you forget?"

He looked from side to side and then up at me, as though to say *There's no one else here,* before jumping onto the seat.

"We're going to drive the route Holly's mom takes to work every day. What do you say to that?"

He sniffed the air, searching for a scent.

"Don't worry. You won't be seeing Holly for a while, dog. You can relax in peace and quiet."

Friday didn't look like he believed me.

10

With Maddie out of the picture while she visited family back home, I was left to my own devices with the Franklin case. And, she left her favorite and only dog behind. She must have thought I could take care of him on my own. I think Friday was still reserving judgment on that. We weren't going on any of our promised daily walks.

"We'll walk when we get back, dog." Friday's ears perked up and he settled into the Packard's front seat beside me.

I powered down the Packard's top before referring to my notes. Franklin gave me the streets his wife normally drove to work. I was familiar with them. Two would be congested at the time she traveled them in the morning.

I made for the first and by late afternoon we were cruising. Traffic was mostly in the opposite direction, headed home. I got onto the second, with the same result.

"Our client's wife was late getting off to work." I found myself addressing a dog. "She would have been looking for a route around the early morning congestion. Since she drove it every day, she'd know where to turn well in advance."

Friday didn't say anything. Maybe be agreed with me.

Maybe he didn't.

"The only way to find out is if we drive the side streets. We'll zig and zag and see what we can see."

I was sure more than a few people would have the same idea. Even with fewer cars during after-hours traffic, it was a pain. Back and forth. Left and right. Crossing streets and taking up on the other side. It was time-consuming and frustrating.

"We're almost done, Friday. What do you say we walk the last few streets? We'll get our exercise and do some investigating at the same time."

He woofed assent. I poured a jug of water and let him bury his face in it. He finished, and I attached his long leash. We were off. Out of the convertible and the wind, it was a lot warmer and definitely humid.

I allowed Friday to take the lead. He tugged at the leash, doing his usual sniffing and snuffling and stopping and starting. He even took time to anoint a fire hydrant. "Good dog, Friday," I told him. "I've wanted to do that a time or two myself."

My shirt was wet and soaked in perspiration. Friday's tongue was hanging out. He was panting a little too hard for my liking. We crossed the street and retired to a restaurant's small sidewalk patio, where we found welcome shade beneath an umbrella.

The waitress appeared and I requested water for two. She took one look and it turned dirty before she disappeared. The dirty looker returned with two tiny glasses.

"Can I get a bowl, please? I like to slurp my water when it's hot like this."

She shook her head and mumbled something about customers and I ignored her until she returned with the requested bowl. I serenaded her with a tuneless ditty for her efforts. She didn't crack so much as a smile. Perhaps it was my singing. Or maybe it was late in her day.

I poured Friday's drink into the bowl and placed it in front of him. While he was lapping up his drink, I wandered to the edge of the sidewalk to have a gander up and down the street.

"Friday, that looks like what we're searching for."

We rushed past the till. The waitress hurried to our table. I was certain she wanted to see if we left the salt and pepper behind.

"Friday. Heel."

He did as ordered, and I halted us a block down the street. The truck was parked at a sharp angle facing the curb. It wasn't quite parallel to the street, as though it was forced into stopping. I led Friday behind a hedge and scanned the street. There was a sedan parked half a block from the truck. Windows down. Someone in the driver's seat. A stakeout, maybe.

"Come on, Friday. We have some scouting to do."

11

I allowed Friday to take the lead, letting him tug me along. We strolled past the car. Music blared. A man occupied the driver's seat.

Behind us a door slammed. Friday halted and looked. I followed his lead. A man carrying a brown bag and a thermos made for the car. He climbed in and the driver left the scene.

We carried on to the Franklin's truck. Took our time getting to it. From a distance it looked to be an immaculate restoration. The colors matched Sandy's description and the pictures he showed me. Both windows were down. I ordered Friday to stay and put on a pair of gloves before opening the driver door.

Inside was a different story. It was a beater, and it needed plenty of work. The dash was cracked and faded in too many places to count. The shift lever indicator was in reverse. I wiggled it to no avail. It was jammed. Missing door panels revealed the window guts. I tried the hand cranks. They worked, but with some difficulty. A window slipped out of its track.

I checked the visor. The ash tray. Under the floor mat. No keys.

A colorful blanket covered the seat. I slipped my

fingers along the crease. They touched something. I dug deeper and came up with a USB drive. I put the dongle back and took pictures. I put the drive in a plastic bag and put it in my pocket before closing up the truck. I took some distant shots. If it got towed, I'd have a record.

I made sure to include the plate. I made sure to check my notebook, too. The plate was definitely a match, but by then there was no doubt.

"It looks like we found it, dog. Just where we thought it would be. Angela must have turned off the crowded street to make time and ended up waylaid by person or persons unknown. Does that sound official or we aren't a detective team." It wasn't a question that needed answering.

Friday looked up at me. He didn't appear impressed.

Whatever the kidnappers wanted, it wasn't to steal the truck. It might have looked pristine on the outside but for a tailgate filthy with oily exhaust fumes. Inside, it was anything but. Under the hood it was surely a disaster in the making.

"Let's call it a day and head home, Friday. We have some thinking to do."

12

I put in a call to Don Boyle, a friendly lieutenant in the local PD. He was out. I left a brief message about the case and the found vehicle particulars. Even though Sandy's wife wasn't missing long enough to file a report, it never hurt. In this case, the found truck tended to send a message that Angela Franklin could have been abducted.

Next on the agenda was a call to Sandy, Angela's husband. He picked up immediately and I filled him in. "I also found a USB storage drive in the truck. What would you like me to do with it?"

"Could you bring it over? It's late to try to find a sitter at this hour."

"I'll feed and water Friday and we'll be there in a bit."

"Holly is going to be so surprised," he said. "She was just asking about Friday a few minutes ago." He mimicked his daughter's name for the dog and chuckled. I did, too. In the background, I heard *Fwiday, Dada? Fwiday?"*

Friday would be in for a shock when Holly showed up to answer the door. No doubt Holly would be, too.

Boyle returned my call just as Friday and I were departing the office. I was pleasantly surprised when he told me he'd already sent a couple of his guys to look over the truck. I wanted to tell him about the USB stick, friends that we were, but I thought better of it until I had Angela's husband look at it.

"Thanks, Don. My client will appreciate it, I'm sure. I owe you one."

"No problem, Nash. Keep me updated, all right?"

I said I would and Friday and I headed for the car. Friday, always one for a ride, jumped right in and took the front seat where Maddie usually sat.

"I miss her too, dog. Maybe we'll get a call later. Wouldn't that be nice? What do you think?"

We arrived at the Franklin residence. Friday followed me to the door and stood by my knee. His nose tested the air. He seemed unsure, but his tail wagged and it looked to me like he was smiling.

"Sit, Friday."

He looked up at me with a quizzical expression before doing as he was told. Maddie had trained him well. A commotion behind the door had Friday perking up his ears. His tail stopped sweeping the step.

"Open the door, dear. There's someone who wants to see you." Sandy's voice filtered past the closed door.

"Who, Dada?"

I imagined the pink-faced little girl looking up at her father.

"Pull it open. You'll see."

The door eased open and short pink fingers slipped out from behind to pull it all the way. Holly's eyes widened. Her mouth opened. Nothing came out. Friday stood up. His nose was even with Holly's. Friday's tongue swiped the little girl's chin. Shocked, she fell back and landed on her rear. She was speechless for only a surprised moment.

"Fwiday! Dada. Fwiday. Look." Both arms waved and pointed at Friday.

Dutiful dog that he was, Friday walked behind her. Holly's head swiveled as far as it could in one direction. She regrouped, and turned the opposite way. Her arms waved. Friday did his duty. He grabbed her little hoodie, pulled her up, and allowed her to settle on two unsteady legs and feet. A huge grin appeared on the girl's face.

"Good doggie, Fwiday. Come. Come."

Friday looked up at me and waited. I gave him a sign and he obeyed. Holly grabbed Friday's collar vest to steady herself. Side by side the pair slowly walked down the hall to what I presumed was the girl's room. Friday's tail wagged so hard I thought it would fall off.

"You gave him a signal," Sandy said.

"Yes. His mistress trained him to respond to certain unspoken signals. If he doesn't see it, he won't go. I think it's good for everyone concerned. If you don't mind, I'll just go down and take a quick look.

"Go ahead. I'll make coffee."

I nodded and made my way down the hall. I passed open doors and looked in rooms. Neat. Tidy. Plenty of pictures of the family. The girl's room was full of stuffed animal refugees and lots of colors and posters and drawings on the walls.

"Do you think you'll be all right, Friday?"

I don't think Holly heard me. She was too busy hugging and petting Friday. The dog was by now resigned to his fate and couldn't be bothered to woof a complaint. Truth be told, he seemed to be enjoying the attention.

I guessed I wasn't the only one who missed Maddie.

13

I handed Sandy the portable drive. He disappeared to retrieve a laptop before settling in at the kitchen table and inserting the USB stick. "It's password protected," he said. I'll be right back."

He returned with a folded piece of paper. He laid it flat on the table. It contained groups of numbers followed by long lists of symbols.

"How secure is that if you write down all your passwords?" I wanted to know.

"Oh, don't worry. It's meaningless unless you know the correct combinations. We do it that way so we can keep everything available in case something happens."

"Well then, I guess this is the case. Something has happened."

He looked up before going to work on the keyboard. It took several tries, but Sandy ended up unlocking the laptop. He went to work on the many folders. Each was locked with a different password.

"Success. I'll get a bigger monitor. It'll be easier on the eyes."

I poured a coffee and went to check on Friday and Holly. The girl was busy chatting away to Friday.

"Bouncy ball, Fwiday. Bouncy ball." She busied

herself leading Friday to the door. He paused halfway through and waited while his playmate rolled the ball. She chased after it and walked it back, halting in front of Friday. He took the initiative and used his nose to send the ball sailing down the hall. Laughing and giggling, Holly chased after it and brought it back.

He nosed the ball again and looked up at me, as if to say I don't think this is how it works, but I'm going with it anyway. His playmate waved her arms in a frenzy. She chased after the ball on her stubby little legs, retrieved it, and waited. I left the pair alone. Holly would end up sleeping well tonight.

I returned to the kitchen. Sandy was busy at the laptop. Fingers flew over keys. Documents launched and he arranged them in overlapping order. "Take a look at this."

I looked, but it was something I was unfamiliar with. Games. Specifically, computer-based games. At least, that's what I got from the letterhead.

"Those are the most recent files according to the time stamps on them. It has to be what she was working on for the presentation. A video game company. Some of those games are real money-makers."

"Do you know the firm?"

Fingers began anew. Sandy brought up a file filled with recent articles about the company. "See these last two? It looks like the company is teetering on the brink of bankruptcy. If they're to be believed, that is."

"You're certain?"

"Oh yes." He changed the search terms and more sites came up, essentially saying the same. "They're all gamer sites. The reporters are highly regarded in the gaming industry."

"Could there be some animosity between programmers and owners?" I asked.

"Oh yes. Quite often."

I wanted to know how.

"The owners want to release the game to start getting a return on their massive investment of time and money. The programmers don't want to release until they think it's ready. Often, the feeling is that it's never ready."

"Is Angela's report there?" I asked.

"If it is, I can't find it. She might have it hidden. I'll need more time."

I went back to check on Friday. He was curled up on the floor in Holly's bedroom. Holly was snuggled up with her face in his neck. Curly red hair stuck out, tickling the dog's wet, twitching nose. Both were fast asleep.

"You better take a look, Sandy."

He halted in the doorway. "I'll be right back." He returned with his phone and snapped a picture. "I'll send you a copy."

I was going to tell him not to bother but thought better. Maddie would get a kick out of seeing Friday all tuckered out by her dog's red-haired little playmate.

"You and Friday might as well head home, Detective Nash. I'm going to be a while figuring this out. When I have it I'll let you know."

14

I turned over the ringing phone. I grinned, recognizing Maddie's number. The smiling woman could barely talk past her own grin. I was relieved she was checking in.

"So, does our girl miss us, or is it my breakfast cooking you miss? I'm frying up a couple of slices of bacon to mix with Friday's breakfast.

"He's getting bacon? How come?" It sounded like a scolding was coming.

"We had a late night last night. Our new client kept us up until Friday couldn't keep his eyes open."

"The client must have come in after I left."

"Late in the afternoon. She's only twenty or twenty-four—"

Maddie didn't allow me to finish.

"What? That young? What's she doing there? Isn't she kind of young to hire a private investigator? What happened? Did her boyfriend stand her up for prom or what?"

"Hang on. Your favorite dog's breakfast is almost ready." I let her suffer while I prepped Friday's breakfast bowl.

Friday wasn't tuned in to the fact I was talking to his mistress. His tail wagged eagerly, anticipating what was coming. I picked the bacon out of the pan and patted it dry. He sensed I was chopping something it to mix in with his breakfast, and his tail continued its furious wagging.

"There you go. Enjoy, dog."

His tail halted and he buried his furry face in breakfast. I went back to my conversation with Maddie.

"Oh, no. Nothing like that. She's—"

"She's what?"

Maddie sounded filled with regret she left on her trip home.

"I'll send you pictures. Friday's in them, too. You'll get a kick out of the pair. They played bouncy ball last night. It plumb tuckered out the pair of them."

I knew better than to wait longer than a minute after we hung up. I wished I could see Maddie's face when she learned the teenager was twenty months old. Or two years—what did I know? I didn't have long to wait.

You are a bad bad man

A phone call interrupted my fun. Sandy managed to unlock his wife's report and was inviting me over to see it. In turn, I invited him to the office. I finished feeding and watering Friday and leashed him for our walk.

"Your girlfriend is coming over, dog."

He looked up at me, head tilted, unsure what to make of it.

"You remember. Holly. Bouncy ball girl."

He woofed and shook his head.

"How soon we forget. Come on. We don't have much time for our walk."

When Sandy and Holly arrived, I was pretty sure her scream of delight could be heard a block away. Holly greeted her *Fwiday* like it was old home week. Sandy fished the bouncy ball out of his backpack and the little girl took over from where she left off the night before. Friday, accustomed to her game of backwards fetch, played along. He happily nosed the ball while Holly chased after it, only to retrieve it and put it down in front of him.

"I wonder how long it's going to take her to train Friday to fetch?" I asked.

"I'm not sure, but I think Friday is smarter than your average dog. He's keeping Holly too happy and busy for her to even think about letting him fetch the ball."

I had to agree with Sandy about that.

"Okay, so what's the latest? Any more phone calls?" I wanted to know.

"Yes. Another shortly after you left. I got to talk to Angie again, briefly. She says she's safe."

That bit was a relief. "Any clue as to what they want? Did they make any demands?"

"They want her report. I told them I didn't have it," Sandy said.

"It wasn't on the laptop. What about the portable drive?" I asked.

"It had a hidden partition on it," he said. "The report is on the partition."

"So then, your wife had an inkling her report was sensitive to a certain business."

Sandy thought for a moment. "I'd say so, yes. It's her job to know that, after all."

"When you talked to your wife again, did you hear any noises in the background? Anything?"

"No. I remembered you asked about that the first time, and I was paying attention. There was nothing."

"What do you know about the company mentioned in the report?" I asked.

"Well, that's the thing. I think I recognized a voice on the other end."

We had a break. Maybe. "Are you certain?"

"Yes. Someone I worked with a while ago. A long while. He was always looking for the easy way. A good coder. But lazy, you know? Resting on his laurels. Not putting out one hundred percent. But good just the same."

It was quiet in the office. I looked around for Friday. The game of fetch had moved to the hallway. Holly was giggling. Something sounding like a ball bounced down the stairs. The giggling halted and the girl cried out.

"Bouncy ball."

Sandy stood up. His chair flipped backwards. He flew to the door. Holly screamed. I followed Sandy. Friday had the hoodie gripped in his teeth. He was fighting to hang on. Holly was on the second step. A look of concentration was fixed on her face. Her tongue was out, curled to the side. She wanted more than anything else to back down those steps and find bouncy ball for Friday.

Sandy reached past Friday for his daughter. The dog released her into his arms. Stubborn Holly twisted her head, searching for the ball.

"Good boy, Friday. Good boy."

Friday looked up at Sandy. Holly called out. "Good boy, Fwiday."

Friday's tail wagged so hard I thought he would shake it off. Sandy put the girl down on the floor and she wrapped her arms around the dog's neck. "Good boy, Fwiday."

As though Maddie herself had said the words, Friday walked a circle around the little girl wagging his tail. He stopped to nuzzle her and sat down. Holly's nose found his and he licked her face.

"Watch her while I get the ball, please."

Sandy returned with the ball and made sure to close the door. As though nothing had gone wrong, the pair began their antics with the ball all over again. Holly busied herself doing the fetching. Each time she brought the ball back, Friday's tail wagged so furiously I thought he'd knock the girl down.

Finally, Friday had enough. Each time he nosed the ball in Holly's direction, he edged closer to his bed. When the girl returned, he nosed her over and she plopped down on her rear on the bed. Friday curled up beside her. She leaned to pet him and fell over.

In minutes the pair were sleeping like puppies sharing a sunbeam.

15

Before the commotion, Sandy talked about hearing a familiar voice. We had a lead, finally. My first thought was to involve Boyle and the police. Angie was a kidnap victim. He'd need to know.

"How do you feel about talking to the police?" I asked Sandy.

Sandy's phone rang, and he held up a hand to wave me off before mouthing the word *Office*. He listened intently before hanging up. "They want to involve the police, too. What do you think?"

"I think we should find out where your guy is and go from there. If he has her, a stakeout should tell us. What do you think?" I wasn't asking for Sandy's permission.

Sandy's only concern was for his daughter. "I won't be able to get a sitter in the middle of the day."

"Between the four of us that shouldn't be a problem."

Sandy looked down at Friday. "If you say so. We're counting on you."

A stakeout with a client. The client's daughter strapped in a car seat. A dog. I needed to have my head examined, and I was the one who suggested it. "Show me where we're going to find this guy, Sandy."

"First things first, detective. Holly?"

The little girl looked up at her father.

"Do you have to pee?"

"No Dada."

She looked at Friday. "Fwiday pee?"

Friday looked from Holly to me. His head tilted. He might have rolled his eyes if he could.

"I don't think Friday needs to, Holly. If he does, he'll let us know, okay?"

Without a car seat in the Packard, we paraded out to an expensive SUV. Somebody was raking in the big bucks. Sandy placed Holly in her car seat. She called out *Goodbye Fwiday* so many times I wanted ear plugs. Friday was all ears, of course. He wasn't fatigued by the girl's attention just yet.

With Holly's cars seat in place, it was time for Frida to get in. "Okay, Friday. Your turn."

He jumped into the back and Holly called out.

"Car wide, Fwiday."

A fawning Friday licked her cheek and settled in beside the girl in the car seat. Dog and little girl busied themselves looking out the window at the passing sights. Sandy powered down the back window on Friday's side and the dog stuck his head out. His ears flapped in the wind. Holly giggled.

Friday brought his head in and looked across at me. I think he had a doggie smile gracing his furry black face. He licked Holly's cheek again before sticking his head into the fresh air. Friday's tail flicked back and forth. Holly giggled again and tried to grab it.

I trusted Sandy's judgment to get us to the kidnappers. I trusted that he knew who they were. I trusted him to remain in the car with Holly and Friday. Maybe I was a little too trusting. I didn't have anything else to go by. He slowed and signaled a turn.

"That's the house. The green one. With the white door."

"Don't stop. Drive past." I didn't turn to look as we went by the house on my side of the car. "Go around the block. This time park before you get to the house."

I waited for Sandy to get back on the street.

"Park there, on the right. It'll give us a clear view of the place." I waited until he shut off the ignition. "Sandy." I addressed him.

He looked at me and then at his daughter in the back seat. Even Friday brought his head in and was looking.

"Don't look at Holly. Look at me."

He looked. Holly looked. Friday looked.

"Listen to me. You will not get out of the car. You will stay in the car with Holly and keep her safe. You will not let Friday out of the car. Is that understood?

He nodded.

"Nodding isn't good enough. Say it back to me."

He repeated my instructions, and I was good to go. I felt for my automatic beneath my jacket. Sandy noticed.

"Is that necessary?" he asked.

I didn't answer right away. I slipped the gun from the holster. Slipped the magazine. Checked it. Replaced it with a satisfying click. Chambered a round and re-holstered.

"Yes. It is. It's as necessary as it is for you and Holly to remain here with Friday to stay safe."

I had a car-load of civilians. Friday was the only one I knew for sure would obey me. The other two were at the whim of the adult parent. And with Sandy's wife in the house and me with a loaded gun, I figured for sure he'd be running toward the place the minute I disappeared. If he did, I was counting on him leaving his daughter in the car with Friday.

"Friday. Stay with Holly.," I instructed.

Friday's ears perked up and he snorted. I took that for a yes.

16

I eased out of Sandy's SUV and checked the quiet street a second time. Leaves rustled in a gentle breeze under bright sunshine. Given the time of day, anyone going to work was already on their way. No one on exercise routines pushed carriages or jogged. I slipped hands into both pockets, nonchalantly strolled across the street, and made for the house.

I looked before climbing the steps to the front porch and the door. A curtained window on each side prevented me from seeing inside. Faint voices drifted through an open window. A woman, arguing with a man. Something about never getting financing now, thanks to someone's stupidity.

I didn't wait to hear more. I left the front and walked around to the back of the house. It was well kept. A picnic table. A sandbox and a child's swing. By the look of it a family house. Sandy's truck was parked in the back yard beside a garage off the alley. The kidnappers must have moved it, probably hoping the police wouldn't find it.

I eased up to the screen door. The main door was open. I overheard a second male saying something about being stupid to try something like this. The same woman's voice did an *I told you, when you forced me out of the truck.*

Two males. A woman. Presumably Sandy's wife, Angela. I heard enough to begin to wonder if the woman might be in on her own kidnapping. I never broached the subject with her husband. Now it appeared to be a possibility.

I needed to hear more. I crouched beside the door and settled in with my hand on the holstered automatic. Friday barked once, followed by a loud, sharp squeal. A door slammed shut. Had the fool husband got out of the SUV?

Sure enough, the front door to the house banged closed. Sandy's panicked voice floated through the open back door.

"Why did you take her? You had the information—"

He stopped talking in a hurry. I had what I needed. My hand switched from the holstered automatic to the leather sap in my pocket. The hinges squeaked on the cheap screen door and the spring stretched and twanged. I held it while it slipped closed on its own.

Loud voices arguing in the front of the house drew my attention like a magnet. I eased past the kitchen and halted at the doorway. Two men I didn't recognize were having a heated discussion concerning the merits of kidnapping Sandy's wife when they already had her report.

Sandy and Angela shouted so loud it drowned out the other two. I listened and wondered if Sandy's daughter was still in the car with Friday. To that end I took out my sap and connected with stranger number one. He dropped like a rock in the middle of a lake. Number two shut up and made for the front door, fast.

I wasn't quite so fast. He double-timed it for Sandy's SUV. Sandy's anxious voice confirmed my suspicion.

"Holly is still in it!"

Wanting to get to the guys before they spilled the beans, he tossed the key fob.

"With the windows up, no doubt."

He looked from me to his wife. "I take it this is Angela?"

I waited, not in the least concerned for the car and Holly. My patience was rewarded when I heard a fierce growl and sudden barking.

"It sounds like Friday is doing his job. What about you, Sandy? Where do your loyalties lie? With the kidnappers, or with your family?"

I made for the street and Holly. Friday was holding the kidnapper by a pant leg and he wasn't about letting go.

I called to the dog. "All right, Friday. Heel."

Friday's jaws opened. The man's leg jerked free. He lost his balance and fell backward. Angela scooped up Holly while I brought out the handcuffs. The little girl jumped for joy.

"Mommy. Mommy. Fwiday is hurt. He got a owie. Dada slammed the door. It hit Fwiday." Holly was about to burst into tears knowing Friday was injured.

"Don't worry, Holly. I'll take Friday to the doctor. You go with your mom, okay? Friday will be fine, I promise."

We did brief introductions. I told Angela who I was and why I was there. She thanked me on behalf of herself and Holly.

"What do you want to do with these two, Mrs. Franklin?"

"I'm going to have words with my husband. Do you have a card?"

I handed her one and asked her to come into my office when she could.

I called Boyle to let him know I had the kidnappers in custody. He would be sending a car. I left out Sandy's part in it until I heard from his wife. It wasn't up to me to become involved in a domestic matter. I knew how those could go, and it wasn't always good for someone who stuck their nose where it wasn't wanted.

Judging by the looks Angela was giving Sandy, I knew it wasn't over, either. Holly was happy to be in her mother's arms again. Even Friday, limping and in pain, seemed happy. I wouldn't be happy until I got him to the vet.

"All right, Holly. I'm taking Friday to the doctor. You can come visit him whenever you want, all right?"

She wrapped her arms around the dog's furry neck. His cold nose connected with her bare skin. She giggled and waved and called out. "Goodbye Fwiday. Get better. No more owie. Goodbye Fwiday."

Angela picked up her daughter. "I'll be calling your office, detective."

"By all means. I'll be expecting it."

I located the keys for the truck and waited for a badly limping Friday, favoring his right foot. I wasn't happy to see the dog in the condition he was in. He was obviously in pain. I helped him get into the truck.

"We're going to see Dr. Hannah, Friday. Do you remember Dr. Hannah?"

He whined and I winced, suspecting how much pain he was in.

I made the call while wrestling with the steering and the brakes and the shift lever. Eventually, we made it through traffic without doing damage. I waited for Friday, sniffing and snuffling and limping his way into Dr. Hannah's office.

The woman's soothing voice did its usual number on both of us. She felt and prodded and poked and x-rayed. Friday and I both remained remarkably calm for the duration, even with the pain Friday was obviously suffering.

She showed me the x-ray and pointed out the damaged leg. "There's nothing broken. It's tendons, mostly. And a very bad bruise. It's going to take time to heal, though. He has to stay off that leg. No stairs, up or down."

Dr. Hannah bound his right leg and repeated strict orders not to allow him to go down any stairs until she saw him again.

"Friday is going to be very stiff and sore tomorrow."

She stroked his back and handed me painkillers while giving detailed instructions on how to feed them to him and how often. I paid attention. If I killed Friday with painkillers, I knew Maddie would kill me, and there would be no painkillers for me, either.

She printed out the instructions for me and we said our goodbyes. I carried Friday up to the second floor. I debated whether to take him all the way to the apartment on the third. I nixed it and ended up putting him to bed in the office.

I retrieved blankets from the closet and made up the sofa. He seemed relieved that I was going to stay with him.

He slurped a little water before his eyes fluttered and he fell into a deep sleep, thanks to the drugs.

The first order of business was a call to Maddie. She picked up right away and I filled her in on Friday's injuries. Initial panic was replaced with concern for her dog.

"Are you coming home?"

She didn't answer, so I told her about the x-ray revealing no broken bones. The sore tendons. The swelling and bruising. About how confident I was in Dr. Hannah's diagnosis.

"Is my dog dying?"

"Not on my watch, lady. Dr. Hannah gave us painkillers. I'm sleeping on the office sofa with Friday. He's drinking and eating. I'll be carrying him downstairs. If it's too much for him, I'll carry him back up.

"In that case I'll be home on the weekend. If I don't arrive, you know where the jail is in that town I have to pass through."

And I knew she'd be calling the doctor the instant we hung up, but I didn't mind. I'd be doing the same thing were it me.

"We're going back to the doctor again tomorrow. We'll file a full report on the results."

Friday forlornly wagged his tail and held up his bandaged leg for the camera. He generally looked sad and inconsolable. He whined a goodbye and I hung up. He knew how to play the injury card when it came to his mistress, that's for sure. I sent pictures off to Maddie. I made sure the made-up sofa was in the background with Friday.

I got up a couple of times during the night to check on Friday. I sat beside him and petted and stroked and ruffled his ears. I gave him a treat and one of Doctor Hannah's pain killers and waited for him to fall asleep before going back to the sofa.

Breakdown

I texted Maddie to let her know I was taking care of her Friday. It was a surprise that she wasn't calling every hour.

It was days before I heard from Angela Franklin.

18

I cut the injured Friday a lot of slack. I made sure he had water and food and painkillers. I carted the heavy dog up and down the stairs and was glad I hadn't put him up in our apartment and another flight. I slept with him and made sure he knew I cared and worried over him.

He wagged his tail, albeit slower than usual. He snuffled and whined and yawned and scratched the floor with his good paw when he wanted some attention. I made sure to give him plenty, even when he didn't scratch the floor.

Maddie called. I called. She let me know she talked with the vet both times after our visits with Dr. Hanna. I didn't mind. It gave her peace of mind and allowed her to stay with her family for as long as she planned.

Angela Franklin came to visit on the third day. Holly's familiar voice rang out from the bottom of the stairs and I smiled.

"Fwiday upstairs, Mommy."

Friday's ears perked up and his tail wagged cautiously at the sound of the little girl's voice. I knew he wanted to get up to greet her. I wouldn't let him.

"Friday's been waiting for you, Holly."

"Down, Mommy, down *pwease.*"

Her feet hit the floor and Holly waddled toward Friday. His ears perked up and his tail wagged. When she got close she got down on all fours and crawled the rest of the distance. They faced each other nose to nose. Friday licked her chin and Holly giggled. "Look Mommy. Fwiday has a boo-boo." She wrapped her arms around his neck and hugged.

"Careful of his leg, honey."

"I will, Mommy."

I was grinning so hard I though my face would break.

"He's getting better, Holly. He's a lot better now that you're here. He was waiting to see you."

"Is Fwiday sick?" she wanted to know.

"Well, like you said, he has a boo-boo. But it's getting better. We visited Friday's doctor—"

"Fwiday has a doctor? I have a doctor too," the little girl declared. "Don't I mommy?"

"Yes, he does. We visited her yesterday. She said to tell you Friday is getting better every day.

"Don't worry, Fwiday. I won't sit on your boo-boo."

I left dog and little girl to commiserate and addressed Angela. "Have you made any decisions?"

She sighed before beginning. "I have. Sandy and I are done. He almost cost me my job. The first thing I did after leaving those three was call my boss to explain what happened." She hesitated and I wondered if she left out her husband's part.

"The company was this far from making an offer to those guys. Had I made it into work, we'd have done it based on my report. I even went so far as to declare a conflict of interest before I went to work on the gaming company assignment. The boss wasn't concerned. He gave me full rein to do what I had to do and damn the consequences."

She shook her head.

"They would have been sitting pretty by the end of

the day if they hadn't taken me. As it stands now, they're done. So is their company. So is my husband. No one will touch them after that episode."

She looked from her daughter to me.

"My business partner will be back on the weekend. If we can do anything for you and Holly, let us know. Maddie isn't known to any of them. If you need her for anything, she's available. We're both available."

She stood up and retrieved Holly. Friday sat up and held up his injured leg, looking for more sympathy before the pair left.

"One more thing. Your husband left a check." I pulled it out of the file and handed it to her. She took a quick look.

"Oh for crying out loud. He didn't even bother to fill in an amount. Thank you for being so diligent, Mr. Nash. How much do I owe you? I want to pay for Friday's doctor bills, too."

"When Maddie gets back, I'll let her know. In the meantime, if you need us, call."

"Come on, Holly. It's time to say goodbye to Friday."

The little girl called out *Goodbye Fwiday* all the way down the stairs. Friday gingerly got up and limped to the top of the steps and barked. Looking for all the sympathy he could muster, he waved his injured paw in Holly's direction. Holly didn't stop waving and Friday didn't stop barking until she disappeared.

"Well, Friday. I guess that's all the excitement for one day. Were you happy to see Holly?"

He woofed and wagged his tail while limping his way back to bed.

"It's been a long day. We both need a nap."

I stretched out on the sofa and closed my eyes. In a minute I sat up. "Friday," I called to the dog. "I have a better idea than this setup."

19

Maddie drove like a demon through the night to get home to the two favorite males in her life. She arrived exhausted at first light. She quietly climbed the stairs to the second-floor office and eased open the door, expecting to see both of them. The office was empty. There was no water or food bowl, either.

She closed the door and climbed the stairs to their third-floor apartment. She opened the unlocked door and walked in. Friday's bed was empty. There was no one in the living room. She pushed open the bedroom door and lo and behold, discovered Jim in bed under the covers and Friday stretched out beside him.

She ran through the shower and dressed before making for the kitchen to fix breakfast for three. She cleaned up the dirty dishes Jim left behind while he was taking care of her dog. *Taking care of their dog,* she thought now. She finished and headed for the bedroom carrying a tray fit for the kings in her life.

She was unsure how well Friday's leg was healing, even after talking to the vet. She went to the dog first. She knew he'd wake up and want to get close to her. She didn't want him walking on his leg more than he should.

She ruffled his ears and stroked his back and scratched

his neck. Friday woke immediately and stuck his cold wet nose on her arm. It gave her goosebumps.

"How's my good boy? Are you okay, Friday? Did Jim take good care of you?"

Friday snuffled and whined and raised his sore leg to be comforted. "You are such a ham. Someone we both know told me you were healing nicely. Now you're telling me you want even more sympathy. You are a bad dog."

Friday wasn't having it. He nuzzled and licked and poked and whined until he had his mistress laughing uncontrollably. He raised his injured leg for inspection like a soldier proudly saluting.

"Shame on you. Don't go away. I'll be right back."

Maddie returned with Friday's bandana. She tied it round his neck and he stretched and stood on all fours. His head turned to Jim still asleep on the bed.

"Wake Jim up. Good dog."

Friday stuck his cold nose against Jim's warm neck. Jim stirred and pulled the covers over his bare neck and mumbled, barely awake. "Zelda. Don't do that. I'm trying to sleep."

Friday barked and did it again. Jim opened an eye and looked out from beneath the blanket. He rolled upright and sniffed. "Oh. Friday. It's you. When did you learn to make coffee?"

Friday pranced on the bed, climbing over Jim to get to Maddie. The dog felt it necessary to let her know he was happy to see her all over again.

"When did you get here?" Jim wanted to know. "Is that breakfast I smell? Take the *Help Wanted* sign down. You're hired."

"First things first." Maddie placed Friday's bowl on the floor in front of him and helped him onto the floor.

"Now you. Dig in before I change my mind and throw it out."

While dog and man filled stomachs with hearty

breakfasts, I regaled Maddie with tales of Holly. How she fell on her tush. How Friday rescued her and helped her up. About almost going head-first down the stairs. About how concerned the little girl was when she saw Friday's bandage and his boo-boo.

"She sounds like a real character. How old is she again?

"Eighteen or nineteen. I told you already. You thought she was a teenager, remember?"

Maddie blushed a bright pink. Friday nosed her thigh and held up his paw.

"Friday, I thought you were healed. Are you still looking for sympathy? Didn't Jim give you enough love?" Maddie asked.

Friday looked up at his mistress with a forlorn expression and dark brown eyes. He nudged her leg again. His head rested on her thigh. She rubbed his snout and scratched at his ears.

"All right. I'll sit with you for a bit. But no faking it, even if you are a handsome boy in that bandana."

Friday pranced all the way to his bed, completely forgetting to limp.

"I knew it. You are faking."

He hung his head, looked guilty, and snorted his embarrassment at getting caught out.

"What's the latest with the case, Jim?"

"I'm waiting to hear from Angela Franklin. I think she wants to get rid of her husband after the kidnapping fiasco. By the look of it, he was in on it with the two jokers who own the company she was investigating."

She looked up from Friday to me, unbelieving.

"I know. They were sitting pretty until they tried to find out what Angela's recommendation was going to be. Now they're just a couple of losers with nowhere to go and no one to do financing. They and their company are done. Sandy Franklin quite possibly along with them."

20

I took out my notes on the case for Maddie to review before heading upstairs for a quick shower. When I returned, she was busy making her own notes.

"Fwiiidaaay." The little girl's sing-song lilt floated up from the lobby to the. "I coming seeee yoooou."

Friday's ears perked up and he got up on all fours. He barked once and sat back down. His head tilted and he listened to Holly's short little footsteps on the landing as they approached the door.

"Fwiiidaaay. Come find meeeee."

He pretend-limped his way and cautiously poked his nose past the door's frame. At that instant, Holly, doing the same, stuck her face past her side of the door.

"Peek-a-boo."

Friday's wet, cold nose connected with pink-faced Holly. The little girl giggled and hugged the dog.

"Fwiday has a boo-boo, mommy. Oh." Holly saw Maddie, halted mid-stride, teetered back and forth, and looked up at her. "Hi-hi. Do you know Fwiday?"

"Oh yes, Holly. I know Friday. I know you, too. Jim told me all about you."

Maddie held out her hand and introduced herself to Holly's mom. "I've been reading up on your case. Jim mentioned you might have something more for us."

"Yes. Well. I've been using the time to think about things." Angela Franklin halted before going on. "I'm going to divorce my husband. He betrayed my trust when he hacked into my laptop and turned over my report to his former workmates. I could have lost my job. As it is, I'm going to have to work on building up that trust all over again. It's something I don't need."

"If there's anything we can do—" Maddie began.

"Come to think of it, there is."

Holly plopped down on her rear. She called to the dog. "Ups Fwiday. Ups."

I couldn't stifle the grin. "Watch this, you two."

Friday walked behind Holly. In his haste to play her game, he didn't remember to limp. He seized the back of the hoodie in his teeth and lifted Holly off the floor. He lowered her on both feet and let go. Holly turned and hugged his furry neck before abruptly plopping down again.

"Fwiday. Ups."

Friday was no stranger to this game. He wasn't having any of it. He stretched out on the floor beside the little girl and nudged her. It convinced her to do the same before she buried her face in his neck and giggled.

"Furry Fwiday. Boo-boo gone."

His ears perked up and he looked up at Maddie.

"I knew it, Friday. You are faking it, aren't you? Shame on you. Even Holly caught you."

The dog stuck a cold nose in Holly's neck to chastise her. It didn't work.

"Fwiday all better now."

I ignored the pair's antics and listened while Angela informed us she didn't want the police involved any more than they had been. She would be letting them know she wouldn't be pressing charges. What she did want was to learn how much her husband had been involved in the kidnapping. It more than likely meant she wasn't set on divorcing him just yet.

"We'll see what we can do. We'll need to know where those two hang out when they aren't kidnapping you."

Angela filled us in on the haunts and hangouts of the two kidnappers. It appeared to be mostly the house they lived in. They programmed and gamed and didn't get out much, by the sound of it.

Satisfied, we let Angela and Holly depart. We did a back-and-forth discussing it, but the only plan we could come up with was for Maddie to go undercover. She would be the one to attempt to find out how involved Sandy Franklin had been in the whole affair. Maddie was gung-ho to go to work.

"It's a smart move on Angela's part. Having a little girl to raise and no husband to stay home and take care of her is quite a bite to chew off."

"I'm actually on Sandy's side in this. You should see how he was with that girl. I hope he wasn't as stupid as he appeared when I walked in on them in that house."

Maddie paced the office floor.

"What's wrong?"

"What does a hacker's girlfriend wear?" she wanted to know.

"I'm thinking plaid. Lots of it."

She looked at me. "How do you know?"

"I don't. I'm guessing. Call Angela and ask her. Just remember that you can't be seen with her."

"Then I'll use my wardrobe. Come on, Friday. We have work to do."

Friday pretended to struggle to get up on all fours. Maddie saw through him like an open window. "You don't fool me, dog. Dr. Holly said your boo-boo is all better."

He looked across the room at me, hoping for support. I shrugged and shook my head. He hung his own and forlornly followed his mistress up the stairs.

It didn't look like it, but we both knew he was happy Maddie was finally home. Half-way up the stairs Friday's tail began its frantic wagging all the way to the landing.

I know, because I checked. There wasn't the slightest evidence of a limp. I called up after him.

"You're not fooling us any more, Friday. Your little playmate spilled the beans on you."

21

It was obvious Maddie missed Friday. It was more obvious that the dog missed her. Within the confines of the apartment, he followed her everywhere. He sat beside her and nudged her with his nose when he felt he wasn't getting the proper amount of attention.

She patted and petted and scratched and rubbed and ruffled his ears. Friday preened and whined and wouldn't stop making self-satisfying noises.

"It's nice to know my dog missed me. How about my man? Did he miss me, too?"

I looked down at Friday. "Well, I don't preen and whine and wag my tail all that much, but yeah. I missed you. I was pretty worried about Friday, though. I was afraid his leg was fractured or worse. We went to see Dr. Hannah—"

At the sound of the veterinarian's name, Friday's ears perked up and he woofed.

"First thing and found out it was only a bad bruise and sprain. She bandaged him up and I took him home and called you."

"I'm glad you did."

"I was really worried. I know you were reluctant to leave him with me."

"He was in good hands. Now get over here. It's your turn to be petted and scratched."

Friday held up his good foot, looking for the last dregs of sympathy from his mistress.

"Yes, I know, Friday. You had a harrowing week. I'm home now. You can relax. You're back on my radar."

That seemed to placate him before Maddie added one last thing.

"And you're holding up the wrong foot."

He must have been embarrassed at being caught out. He made for his bed and sighed before stretching out and closing his eyes.

"Now then, detective. What's the plan for the two stupids?"

It was my turn to look for some sympathy. "I thought we were going to pet and scratch." I was hoping for some placating, too.

"You have something to look forward to later. Let's get started on work."

Maddie went to the closet and returned with her backpack. She hauled out a mess of wrinkled clothes and laid them out on the sofa. "I did a little gaming in my past. My brother was the king, though. He whipped my ass so many times it's still scarred."

"So then, judging by the wardrobe I'm looking at you're good to go."

"You bet. All I need now is to come up with a plausible excuse to find and meet those guys," she said.

22

Maddie **searched through** her old wardrobe and found a t-shirt with a suitable logo and something big and sloppy to wear over it. Loose jeans and white sneakers completed her ensemble. At the last minute she checked her appearance and added a ball cap. She was convinced she'd be able to worm the information she needed out of Angela Franklin's kidnappers.

"All right, James. Good to go. Let's do this."

The pair made for the Packard. Jim stopped at the curb blocks away from the house. "Are you sure this is how you want to work it?"

"What else is there? We need to be quick. If what Angela says is true, they're gullible. Since the kidnapping, they're probably worried sick about repercussions."

"You're right. Putting you in there unannounced just might do the trick. All set?"

Maddie nodded and opened the door. She took off running full tilt. Jim waited for her to disappear, knowing she was right. She had to do it fast. If Angela Franklin changed her mind and told her husband, it would be over before it started. Either she wanted to find out the truth, or she didn't. We had to come up with results.

In Maddie's enthusiasm, she zig-sagged a couple of extra blocks, working up a good sweat in the process. She arrived at the house, out of breath and panting. Perspiration streamed down her face. The front and back of her shirt was soaked.

She bent over, inhaled deeply, and pounded on the front door. She didn't wait for an answer. She immediately ran around the back of the house and began pounding all over again. She used both fists in a rat-a-tat-tat and then halted to listen.

She ran to the front and repeated her actions. She screamed. Kicked at the door. Banged on the windows so hard she thought they'd break. She turned the handle and the door opened. She shoved it wide. It banged against the wall. She ran inside and screamed as loud as she could.

"What the hell?" Two heads poked past the doorway. A male voice rose above the commotion. "Who're you?"

Maddie gasped for air. "Oh thank goodness. I was so scared." She could barely speak.

"What's wrong? Are you all right?"

"I am now. There was a van. A white van—" Breathless, she halted and inhaled noisily. Her chest heaved. She had their attention.

"It stopped in front of me. The door slid open. There were two men inside. I ran around it. I've been running for blocks. Yours is the only door that was open."

"Can we get you anything? Do you want to call anyone? The cops?"

Her breathing became more regular. She was able to speak without effort. "Police? No. I can't. No way." She hesitated and looked from one to the other. "But thanks for offering. I'm good now. No cops, okay?"

She looked at the huge monitor. There was a game on it. One she didn't recognize. She hadn't been a big gamer, but when they were kids her younger brother talked her into playing whenever he could. "What is it? I've never seen it before."

They looked at one another as though trying to decide whether to tell her.

"It's one we designed. Would you like to try it out?"

She was in. "Sure. Do you have something to drink? I'm thirsty after all that running. I'm Maddie, by the way. Who're you?"

"I'm Todd. He's Jeremy."

She felt pretty good. The spur of the moment mention of not wanting the cops involved worked. She saw them look at one another, as though to confirm her judgment concerning the cops. After all, they had their own secrets. They just didn't know she knew about them.

She sat down on the sofa and looked around. Empty pizza boxes were stacked in a corner. The pile was neat, at least, and she presumed they were empty. She sniffed, to confirm it. Empty junk food bags lay scattered beneath the coffee table. Empty soda cans and bottles, too. They were gamers, all right.

"Let's play." She took a breath and made to grab a controller.

One of the guys handed her a headset. "You'll need this."

"Right." She put it on and did a *1, 2, 3 testing* out loud. Was that what they did? She didn't know. She never used a headset with her brother. She picked up the controller again and waited.

They went easy on her in the beginning. Jeremy stood behind her on the sofa and observed before chiming in with helpful hints until she had the gist of the game. Amplified stereo speakers boomed with gunfire and the whoosh of explosions. Grunts, groans, screams and other sounds all came through the headset.

"You're doing good, Maddie. Give him hell."

Breakdown

She wasn't that good. In ten minutes, if it was that long, she was dead and out of the game.

"Make an account for her, Todd," Jeremy told him.

23

It was dark when Maddie remembered to look out the window. "I need a break, guys."

She made her way to the kitchen. The counter was overrun with piled-on dirty dishes. The table was covered in them. Strangely, the sink was empty. She ran water and filled it. "You got any dish soap?"

"Maybe under the counter."

An hour later and the job was done. She returned to her original mission in the kitchen and opened the fridge. No way was she cleaning that mess. She opened the door to the microwave. It was in the same condition. *Christ these guys live like pigs.* No way was she checking out the bedrooms. Bad enough she had to use the facilities. That wasn't as bad as she worried it might be.

"What're we eating, guys? It's late."

The game halted and they looked at her like she was from another planet. "Uhh—"

It wasn't a difficult question. She waited, hands on hips. "We usually phone to get something delivered."

No shit, Sherlock. She knew that by the stack of pizza boxes. "How about Chinese?"

Todd and Jeremy looked at her again. "Chinese?"

"Yeah. You know. Rice and vegetables and soup and

stuff. Fortune cookies. The usual Chinese fare."

They looked from one another to her and back. Apparently that was a new one on them. "All right. We'll try it. You can order."

"You got money?"

Hands went into pockets and came out with wrinkled bills. She counted it out and went to her phone to place the order. She killed time going out to the back yard. The grass was neatly trimmed. Swings and a sandbox filled a corner. When someone yelled about the food she returned to the house and paid.

"I need another ten, guys."

She handed it to the driver and closed the door. They sat around the living room, eating and kibitzing. Eventually conversation lagged, and Todd brought up her refusal to call the police. "What did you do?"

She didn't hesitate. "I shouldn't say. I don't know you. It could get me in trouble." If she was going to get out of this pigsty, she had to do it as soon as possible. Her skin was starting to crawl. She needed a shower just looking around.

"How about if we tell you what we did?"

Maddie couldn't believe what she heard, so she laughed. "You two? You're gamers. Did you SWAT someone you hate?"

Todd and Jeremy exchanged glances. Jeremy went into the kitchen. The escaping gas of three sodas filtered through to the living room. He didn't return right away. Todd turned to her. "Why do you think we're not capable of swatting someone? We could do it if we wanted. We kidnapped someone."

The ease with which the revelation was disclosed put Maddie on full alert. "Who did you kidnap?"

Jeremy returned with the sodas and handed them out. "Did I hear you right? You told her, didn't you?"

Todd's mouth opened but nothing came out when he

realized he made a huge mistake. No doubt Jeremy would be on his case for a week.

"We don't know her, Todd. She could be anybody."

Todd wasn't convinced. "She's just like us. Besides, she said she'd tell us why she didn't want the cops involved with that guy chasing her."

He looked at Maddie. "You're going to tell us, right?"

A noise at the back door drew Jeremy away to investigate. He recognized Sandy carrying Holly. He called out to his friend. "It's all right. It's Sandy."

Maddie tensed immediately. The man was the reason she was in this predicament. She'd never met him. He couldn't possibly know her. She turned to the man in the doorway as he put the little girl on the floor. Holly recognized Maddie immediately and began pointing.

"Dada. Maddie. Fwiday's fwend."

Holly spit out her soother and made for Maddie. "Hi-hi Maddie. Fwiday here?"

Thanks to the little girl, her job was complete. She knew for certain Angela's husband was part of the kidnapping scheme. Exactly what part wasn't obvious yet, even if Sandy didn't need two and two to make four.

"What's she doing here? How did this woman get in? Where did you see her, Holly?"

Holly looked up at her father. "Fwiday. We know Fwiday."

"Dammit you two. We're into it now." Sandy picked up his daughter. "It's time to go, dear. Say goodbye."

Todd and Jeremy made to stand up and follow him out the door.

"Don't leave her alone, you morons. She'll get away."

24

Maddie recognized the trouble she was in the instant Holly remembered her. Her brain raced to figure a way out. She looked around. There was nothing she could use to fight her way out. She didn't think Todd and Jeremy were hard-core criminals. Kidnapping, sure. But even that had been a co-conspirator's wife. She couldn't imagine those two wanting to dump her in a swamp.

It was more than a few hours since she last texted Jim to let him know how it was going. Would he be concerned by now that she hadn't sent another? He'd been reluctant to let her do this job, but she convinced him. After all, the suspects were only nerdy gamers. She even brought up that they only kidnapped Holly's mom, and hadn't harmed the woman in the slightest.

Jim gave in with a sigh and a shake of his head and then reluctantly said yes. Thanks to that, she was in it up to her neck. In fact, it went past her neck when a bag slipped over her head and two pairs of hands pinned her arms to the chair. She struggled to no avail. They were too strong for her.

"Tape her. I'll hold her."

Maddie kicked and fought to free her arms and screamed.

"Don't let her get up."

They taped her arms and wrists, securing her in the chair. Her feet were next. A kick elicited a loud groan before both feet were taped tight to the chair legs. She was a prisoner.

"What are we going to do with her?"

"Don't worry about her. She won't be going anywhere."

Not wanting to antagonize her captors, Maddie held her tongue and remained silent. She recognized the seriousness of the situation she found herself in. The housecleaning she did in the kitchen gained her nothing.

She recognized the sound of drapes being closed. What little light filtered through the hood ceased when the lights were switched off. Doors slammed. A car started. She waited before calling out. No one answered. They were gone. She was alone.

In seconds she was rocking in the chair, back and forth, to no avail. Her back slammed against the chair. She made a feeble attempt at working space between the tape and the chair's arms. The duct tape was too tight and too sticky. It was the same for her feet. She changed tactics and threw her upper body into it by rocking side to side, again and again.

She suffered through a couple of false starts before finding the rhythm. She lost count of the number of attempts, but gravity finally took over and the chair tipped. She slammed onto the floor on her side. Her head banged against something solid and she saw stars before blacking out.

Someone groaned. Was it her? She couldn't remember. No. Wait. She could. Holly. Holly showed up with her father. The hood. And tape. She managed to tip the chair over. Then what? She struggled against her restraints. Couldn't move. She was still tied up. No. Taped. They taped her.

Her head ached. Someone groaned again. It was her. She was the one doing the groaning. Damn but her head ached. She wiggled her fingers. Did the same with her toes. Tried to move her head. It hurt too much.

She opened one eye. Then the other. She couldn't see anything. Remembered the lights were out. Remembered the hood. She sucked in a huge gulp of air and the hood closed over her mouth. Still there.

Well, she was into it now. Had she texted Jim? Once. Twice? She couldn't remember. Would he come to her? What about Friday. She should have brought him. He'd take care of her. But no, she couldn't. Why not? Wait. She knew why. What was it? Why was it so hard to remember?

Thinking was too much for her. She blacked out again.

25

I was reluctant at first to send Maddie on the job. Memories of hauling a former partner out of a drum in the everglades were not that distant. I didn't want something similar happening to Maddie. We talked about it, and she made a point of telling me she'd be texting updates on a regular basis.

"How dangerous can a couple of game-playing computer nerds be, Jimbo?" she had asked.

So yes, I had confidence in her abilities. It didn't mean I was concerned. Which was why I sat on a stakeout a block down the street. I had burritos. I had coffee. I had Friday and a pocket full of treats. How much trouble could Maddie get herself into?

The first text came in and I rejoiced. The second complained about the mess in the kitchen, and I reminded her what a happy little homemaker she was. After that, even Friday noticed the level of tension in the car went down to low. I hadn't heard anything since, and now, together with Friday, I was beginning to become concerned again.

I'd been using a lamp shining through what I knew to be the living room's sheer curtains. When the light went out, I concluded the drapes had been pulled. I took matters into my own hands. I let Friday out and forced him to heel. He followed me to the house and up the front steps. I held out my hand and he halted.

"Wait here, dog. Stay."

He wasn't happy, and he let me know with a cold nose rubbed rapidly against my hand, but he obeyed.

"Good boy, Friday."

I covered my holstered weapon and opened the door to advance into the pitch black darkness. I searched for a light switch. Flipped it on to reveal Maddie sprawled on the floor taped to an overturned chair. Blood pooled beneath her head. Head wounds bleed plenty, but knowing that was no comfort. I checked for a pulse and called to the dog at the same time.

"Friday. Come."

The dog bounded into the house and immediately recognized his mistress in distress. He took up a position at Maddie's feet and growled. I dialed 911 and asked for an ambulance and a squad car before cutting her free. I stretched her out, rolled her onto her side, and placed a cushion beneath her head.

"She's going to be all right, Friday. The doctor is coming."

He must have envisioned Dr. Hannah, because he left Maddie to go on patrol. He sniffed and snuffed his way from room to room. He barked, and barked again.

"What did you find, Friday?"

I didn't get a chance to go and see for myself. The dog strutted his way in my direction, tail held high. His mouth clutched something unrecognizable.

"What's that you've got? Bring it here."

He didn't need to be told. He was in the process of doing it anyway.

Maddie groaned and I knew she would be all right. Friday nuzzled her face with a cold, wet nose and she pretended to laugh it off. I wasn't having it. Neither was Friday. Neither would the sirens wailing in the distance. The ambulance would arrive not soon enough for my liking.

"You hit the coffee table when you rocked the chair over," I told her. "There's plenty of blood, but you'll be okay. Help is on the way, sweetheart. So are the police."

The words were more for my reassurance than anything else. Maddie reached for Friday standing by, but she was too weak to raise her arm. "Good boy, Friday. You did good."

Friday snuffled and worried over her. He nudged her with a cold, wet nose in an attempt at consoling her.

"I'll be okay, Friday. Don't you worry. That's Jim's job."

Friday seemed doubtful. He whined and whimpered and lay down beside his mistress.

"Yes, and Jim and Friday are going to kick some ass as soon as that ambulance gets here. You can count on it."

"He'll want to go with me. You might have a fight on your hands."

Friday looked from me to his mistress.

"When you came to, he went foraging around the house. You'll never guess what he came up with."

"Was it Holly's scent?" she asked. Franklin was here with her just before I got tied up by those two. The cute little redhead with the curly hair blew my cover when she recognized me from the office."

"Not exactly her scent, but close enough. He found her soother. Sandy Franklin is in this up to his neck and beyond. You did good. Well, good except for the bang on the head."

Maddie sighed and I regretted what I said next immediately. "Next time, try harder, will you?"

"Be nice or I'll sic my dog on you, Nash."

The ambulance arrived and Friday stood down to let the attendants load his mistress onto the stretcher. We followed them out the door and Maddie made the dog stay with me. He struggled mightily, dancing back and forth between the back of the ambulance's open door and me. He barked and jumped and fussed, but in the end he obeyed.

Maddie called out just before the doors slammed shut. "Stay with Jim. Good dog. I'll be okay."

Friday whined and looked up at me.

"She'll be fine. We'll go looking for trouble when we're done with the police and their questions."

He barked and sat and waited patiently for the police to finish. It took a while. By the end of it we were both stressed and anxious to hit the pavement.

"All right, dog. Let's go looking for trouble."

He nudged my pocket, checking for Holly's soother. Satisfied, he bounded ahead of me to the car and we headed off to the Franklin residence. I dialed 911 on the way and gave them the address.

Friday bounded out of the car, teeth clenched on Holly's soother. He dropped it at the door and barked before picking it up. I rang the doorbell. Holly stuck her head past the open door and spied her favorite dog.

"Fwiday. Mommy. It's Fwiday."

Friday pranced past the little girl and her mother and halted at Sandy Franklin's feet. He dropped the soother and barked. The man's jaw dropped and his face went white.

"The jig is up, Franklin. The police are on the way. So far, it's kidnapping. I discovered my partner bleeding out in your friend's living room. Friday found Holly's soother. Maddie should be at the hospital by now. Thankfully, I got to the house in time."

Angela Franklin sank into a chair. What she suspected was true. Her marriage was over. She gathered Holly in her arms and Friday sat at their feet, as though on guard. He kept a wary eye on Sandy, as did I.

"It's over, Mrs. Franklin. Maddie will be all right. Your husband's two partners in crime will be charged. I'm waiting for the police to arrive and finish up what you asked me to do."

The squad car arrived. Sandy Franklin ended up loaded into the back. Holly called out sad goodbyes to Friday and we double-timed it to the hospital. I put Friday on his short leash and we approached the information desk. After much consternation, the attendant sent us off to Maddie's room.

We found her in time to witness her flirting madly with a young intern. I dropped the leash and stood back. Friday bounded into the room. He woofed softly and instantly Maddie's attention went from the intern to the dog.

"Friday. How's my boy? Did you help Jim?"

Dog ears perked up and his tail wagged furiously. The intern mumbled something about rounds and used the opportunity to depart.

"Of course you did. Where is my savior, anyway?"

"He's right here watching you flirt."

"Oh I was not," she denied. "I was merely making sure he took good care of me."

"Uh-huh. And now it's my turn. I thought I'd waking you up every hour, but that's old news these days."

She regarded me suspiciously. "How do you know not to do that?"

"I got a full briefing from one of the nurses on the floor. How do you think?"

"They want to keep me here overnight. The bang on the head was a good one, so I'm told."

"In that case, we'll be staying with you. I wouldn't want you running off with that intern to leave us stuck paying the bill."

I turned out the light before taking a chair. Friday settled at my feet and kept a wary eye on his mistress. "Now go to sleep. We'll see you when we see you."

I didn't let on I knew the hour thing was old medicine. I wanted to be there just to annoy her.

27

I stepped out of the hospital leading Friday on his leash. He needed more than a little convincing to desert his mistress, but that wasn't unexpected. He needed a much-deserved bathroom break. So did I—the bathroom break, that is. We'd been cooped up—if that was the way to describe it—in a hospital room with Maddie for hours.

I was nervous and unsettled about allowing Maddie to go undercover to help solve our case. I prepared by setting up on a stakeout to surveil the operation. Had it gone according to plan, she would never know I was there. It didn't go that way, but that's why I was there. I could have found Maddie dead or dying instead of in the unconscious state I discovered her.

It was a chore convincing the woman she needed to get in the ambulance for the trip to the hospital. Friday and I followed shortly after. I witnessed her discussion with the intern in emerg. It was disjointed and fumbling. Words slurred. It was enough to convince me she needed to stay.

Against my better judgment, I forced her to submit. It took a lot of talking and some arguing, too. It didn't hurt that the intern was friendly and cute when she finally noticed him.

I followed the intern's instructions to the letter and

while it wasn't necessary to wake her every hour, I made it my job to do just that. If she wanted to pack up and leave the hospital, I'd be there to convince her otherwise. How hard could it be to make sure the woman stayed until morning? Besides, she needed a brain scan, and there'd be no leaving until it happened, if even then.

The nurses grew accustomed to our comings and goings on the floor. At first they objected to the dog, but I wasn't having any of it. I barged right past with Friday in tow. Their objections eventually turned to smiles and waves. Friday didn't mind. He did his thing by wagging his tail and quietly snuffling at the now familiar greetings called out by the nurses.

Maddie was doing well, too, even if at first she'd been more than a handful and reluctant to accept she would be in overnight. It was more of a precaution than anything else. That, and I insisted on it. She argued and objected and generally made herself a pain until she saw how steadfast I was.

So, there was that. The cute intern helped, too.

Thus Friday and I made our scheduled rounds of the hospital grounds and made to return to the room. In another six hours or so, Maddie would be given a clean bill of health and we'd go home. I'd tuck her into bed for the rest of the day, cook for her, and make sure she really was all right.

At least, that was the plan. As plans go, it was a good one, until Friday and I returned to an empty room. The dog looked from the bed to me and back.

"Bathroom. She needed a bathroom break, too, dog," I said.

We settled into our respective resting places and waited patiently for the sound of running water and an open door. We waited a long time.

Maddie's phone was parked on the tray table, face down. I wanted to check it, but discretion being the better part of valor and all, I decided against it.

"She has to be here somewhere, Friday. She wouldn't up and desert us, even if we both know she hates hospitals and doctors." Friday woofed his support for his mistress.

"Wait here. I'll go ask at the desk."

There was no help there. No one noticed Maddie walking past. I asked for the doctor to be paged, and returned to Maddie's empty room, but for her faithful dog waiting patiently. A forlorn dog ran up and made sure I went for the chair before changing his mind.

28

Friday decided **I** should take action immediately. He nosed me in the direction of the door, wanting to force me into the corridor. I convinced him to wait until the doctor returned. He for one ought to know what was going on. Perhaps Maddie convinced him to release her. More likely, she was out getting her brain scan.

On the off chance, I checked the closet. It was empty but for the hospital gown on the floor. Her clothes were gone. So she had been released. I checked the table again for her phone. Strange she would leave it behind.

The doctor entered the room, looked around, and raised an eyebrow.

"Where is she?"

"She's not here. Did you release her while I was walking Friday?" I asked him.

I got a dirty look for my trouble. "Of course not. She took quite a rap on the head. I wanted to keep her here to see if there would be any signs of amnesia."

"Has she had her scan yet? I thought she might be getting it done now." I hesitated, digesting what I just heard. "Amnesia? What the hell?"

He looked at me and waited, apparently considering whether or not I was worthy of further explanation. Or wondering if I had more questions. I did, but I couched them in a statement while looking unhappily at the doctor.

"My girlfriend and business partner is missing. You'd better explain this amnesia thing to us in plain English."

I looked down at Friday. He was staring intently at the doctor and the dog didn't look so happy, either. I waited for the man to begin.

"Maddie obviously suffered a concussion, a traumatic brain injury. That's not up for debate, as you explained how you found her. Part of the problem is, we don't know how long she was out. Do you know if she's had any previous concussions?"

I had to tell him no, that it never came up. He nodded.

"Not unusual. Concussion effects are usually temporary, but they can include headaches and problems with concentration, memory, balance and coordination."

"So she's wandering around like a drunk in a blackout."

He looked exasperated. "That's one way of putting it, I suppose. She was exhibiting some of the signs. She had one scan. I wanted to do another in the morning. That's why I wanted to keep her overnight."

I wanted to ask how that was working out, but I figured I was as much to blame as he was. She skipped on all three of us, after all. "Is it possible she didn't know why she was in the hospital, and decided to make a run for it?"

"Anything is possible, but yes, it is. She was pretty adamant about not wanting to stay overnight. Or stay at all, for that matter. It's possible she doesn't remember anything about what happened when she got knocked unconscious or why she was in the hospital. That's one of the amnesia symptoms."

Oh great. Not only was Maddie wandering around like a drunk on a bender, she had no idea why. "How serious is this, doctor?"

"It's very serious. She needs to be found."

I had my work cut out. Friday was going to have to help.

"All right, doctor. Thanks for your time. I need to get to work. Come on, Friday. Find Maddie."

The dog bounded out the door. He raised his nose, halted his tail, and took off down the hall. He returned moments later and scooted off in the opposite direction. I ran after him and caught up at the first closed set of doors. I pushed them open and he took off again.

"Good boy, Friday. Find Maddie."

Friday didn't find Maddie, but he did find a discarded lab coat in a stairwell. He lost her at the hospital taxi-stand. I showed her picture to the other drivers waiting around, but no one had any idea. The driver hadn't returned. Worse luck, he was overheard announcing he was going off-shift when he completed the fare he was on.

We were out in the cold. It would mean a trip to the taxi company's head office first thing in the morning. Beyond that, there was nothing I could do. Or Friday, for that matter. We had to settle for our mistress being on the run. From what, neither man nor dog knew.

We headed home. Friday scampered up the stairs to the second-floor office. I let him in and he did his circle check for his missing mistress. I left the door open and we proceeded upstairs. She wasn't in the apartment, either.

"Well, dog, we're going to launch a full-blown search tomorrow. We'll start at the taxi-cab's office first thing."

Neither of us was able to settle down. Friday kept going to the door. I finally left it open, and he wandered up and down the stairs from office to apartment whenever he thought he should, which was often. I wanted to follow him, but I was pretty sure it would only upset him more.

She couldn't call. She had no phone. Sure, she could borrow one for a quick call. If she remembered the number. If she remembered us. From what the doctor said, she might not. Short term amnesia, he called it, thanks to the concussion she suffered at the hands of those game-boy morons.

I never should have let her go undercover. Never should have put her in danger. But it didn't seem like there was any danger at the time. Or so I told myself. Until unknown to her, I staked the house out.

I got up and put on the coffee. Sat around and berated myself for not doing more. Wondered what more I could have done beyond sitting outside the house, on guard. Trouble is, I didn't do such a good job until the lights went out. By then, it was too late.

I slept fitfully. Got up to roam around the empty apartment. Bumped into Friday on his patrol from office and back upstairs to roam the place. He nudged me and licked my hand and sat at my feet and generally we felt sorry for one another. He was good company that way.

Come morning, fed and watered, I loaded Friday into the car and we headed for the cab company's office. I made him wait while I went in and rounded up the driver beginning his shift. He recognized the picture.

"I dropped her at the bus depot."

The bus depot? What the hell? What was that woman up to? Then I remembered the concussion amnesia and started feeling guilty all over again.

"Did she happen to mention where she was going?"

He looked pensive. I hoped for more.

"Come to think of it, she did. She mentioned something about having to find a lost dog."

Oh great. She was looking for Friday and didn't know where to start. It was all my fault after all. I flipped the driver a twenty and Friday and I headed off to the depot.

I couldn't be so lucky that the shift hadn't changed. No one recognized Maddie's picture.

"We're back to square one, dog. Now what?"

He looked up at me as I looked down at him. What a pair we were. To be sure I put Friday on a long leash and allowed him to take the lead as we circled the bus station. Ran up and down alleys. Walked the streets. Nothing. Nada. Not a sign. Not a whiff.

"Let's go home, Friday. It's time." Despondent, I headed for the car. Friday heeled after me. I think he had given up, too.

I called Boyle, hoping he might have some suggestions on where to begin. He was out of the office. I dialed Nancy, his wife, and learned he was off on a fishing trip and hadn't taken his phone.

"If he calls, I'll let him know you're looking. You don't sound good, Jim. Is everything all right?"

I explained what happened and we commiserated for a bit before saying goodbye.

Now I was really at a loss.

30

I had nothing. We had nothing, if I included Friday. No clues beyond the bus station, and I had to wait for the shift to change before returning. It was going to be that kind of day.

Eventually the clock rolled around. I tossed the Frisbee for the last time. Friday retrieved it. He seemed to know. He dropped it at my feet and made for the parking lot. I followed, anxious to get going but not having the four legs to match the dog's frenzied pace.

I had the foresight to have a radio installed in the old Packard with Bluetooth. I no sooner started the engine than it pinged with a number I didn't recognize. I almost didn't answer it.

"Jim?"

"Yeah." I recognized the voice immediately.

"I'm down in Largo.

Right away I knew, thanks to touching base with Nancy. "You're fishing. You left your phone at home so you wouldn't be disturbed by work."

"Right. How did you know?"

"I'll never tell." Neither Boyle nor I were men for pleasantries. With it out of the way, he got straight to the point.

"Are you working a case down this way?" he wanted to know.

"No. Why do you ask?"

The man didn't wait. "I saw Maddie. I didn't recognize her right off. She had a huge purple bruise on the side of her head. A swollen jaw. I figured she was on a case, and I didn't want to blow it by saying anything. Is she all right?"

I explained how she got the bruise. And the concussion. That she'd up and disappeared from the hospital.

"She was walking out of the Crab Shack as I was entering. There's an old hotel just across the street. A bit of a dump. She might be staying there."

"I know the place. It's a shame it hasn't been torn down with all the undesirables hanging out in it."

"Yeah. Too bad."

My phone pinged with another call. I let it go to voice mail.

"We're headed that way now, Boyle. Thanks for letting me know."

"No problem, Nash. I'd stay but I just checked in with the office. I need to get back to the city ASAP. Something about a kidnapping. I hope Maddie is all right."

"So do I."

Friday and I double-timed it toward the causeway and the four-lane highway. At the first red light I raised the roof and got honked at for my troubles and the delay.

"Screw them, dog. There'll be no messing your hair now. We need to make time."

I pulled into the Crab Shack's expansive parking lot in Largo. Boyle's car was gone, but I wasn't expecting him to stay behind for us. I left the windows down.

"Friday. Stay."

In the restaurant I showed Maddie's photo around. No one recognized her, but that didn't phase me. The place was busier than a downtown Miami block on Saturday night. I pocketed my phone and returned to the car. Halfway there, I changed my mind and made to cross the busy highway to the dump of a motel.

I dodged cars and squealing tires and strode purposefully toward the dingy-looking office and its dirty window. A skinny kid with long, greasy hair sat behind the desk. He ignored the cow bell on the door and didn't look up. I tapped the counter to get his attention. Slapped the bell half a dozen times.

The magazine slipped from his lap to the floor and he opened his eyes. I held out the phone and flipped my buzzer and in that same instant I asked the question. "You see this woman here?"

He ignored both and rolled his eyes. "I don't remember. You a cop?" He stood up and I flipped my wallet again. Covered it by thrusting the phone in his face.

"That answer your question? Now, about the woman—"

"Yeah. I seen her. She's in a room about halfway down," he informed me.

"You got a key?"

"We're not supposed to—"

I flipped a twenty across the counter and he tossed a key. "Don't forget to bring it back when you're done."

Eager to get to the room, I forgot about the dog left in the open-windowed Packard across the busy highway. Tires squealed. Horns honked. I looked up and caught Friday racing across the road onto the grass turf fronting the motel.

"Dammit."

Panting from the heat and his furious run, Friday raced back and forth on the walkway fronting the rooms. He halted at number 10. I checked the key.

"Good boy. That's the one."

He barked and stepped back. I twisted the key in the lock. The doorknob popped. Friday shouldered my legs out of the way and bounded into the room, ready to pounce. Trouble was, there was nothing for him to pounce on. The room was empty but for a backpack I didn't recognize.

I did a quick search. Found a toothbrush in the bathroom. A hair brush. I couldn't be certain if it was Maddie's or not. I left the key on the night table. Friday jumped onto the bed.

"Come on, dog. There's nothing for us here."

He lay down on the bed. Didn't want to leave. I coaxed him out and together and we waited for a break in traffic to return to the car.

31

I saw her first. Only a second later, Friday barked and made for the car like a bolt of lightning. He jumped up on Maddie and licked at her chin.

"Well if it isn't my two favorite boys. What took you so long?"

I halted in my tracks, intent on cussing her out. Changed my mind. Changed it again. "If we'd known where you were, we'd have brought cake and candles. Is that your backpack across the street? I didn't recognize it."

"So you're a detective after all. Yes."

"Then let's get it. It's time to go home."

I opened the passenger door to let Maddie in. She pulled back the seat to make room for Friday. He refused, and instead waited for Maddie to get settled before jumping up beside her. There was no way he was going to allow his mistress near a door at this point. I agreed with his instincts before slamming my own door.

"Are you going to tell me about it now, or do you want to wait until we're home safe and sound?"

Maddie's eyes shifted to the radio. As usual, she wanted to avoid answering. "There's a voice mail for you."

Okay, if that's how she wanted to play it. We listened to Angela Franklin's sobbing voice tell us that Holly, her daughter, was missing and presumed kidnapped by her husband.

"For crying out loud. Is that case never going to end? Let's go. We'll pick up your backpack and hit the highway to home."

I beat it across the road and stopped in front of her room. Maddie got out to gather her things. Friday followed close on her heels. I knew exactly what he was doing. I wanted to do the same.

With Maddie and her backpack and watchdog Friday safely on board the Packard, I prepared to leave the motel behind. The black SUV filled my rearview mirror. It was all shiny in the bright sun. It pulled into a spot at the end of the unit. I secretly admired it, but no way in hell would I be replacing the quaint old Packard with one of those any time soon.

The driver's door opened and my jaw dropped. Sandy Franklin stepped onto the ground and slammed the door, only to open the rear door. I caught a glimpse of pink topped by flaming red hair. I reversed in a hurry and blocked the SUV in.

Sandy wasn't so glad to see me. He was all about getting back in his SUV. I drove him one in the gut and smacked his head against the door frame. Holly didn't seem to care.

"Hi-hi. Is Fwiday here?"

"Yes he is. Maddie is, too."

"Dada sleeping?"

I looked down at Sandy. He was curled up in a ball on the ground.

"Yes he is, Holly. Dada is tired. He's taking a nap."

I went through his pockets for a room key and opened the door. I carried Sandy into the room and put him to bed. I called to Maddie. "Get Holly out of the car, will you? She needs to see her father in bed."

She looked over at me, and then at Holly in the back

of the SUV. "Well. Lookie here. We rescued a kidnap victim. All right, I'll take her in and show her."

"Hi-hi Maddie. Where Fwiday?"

Friday bounded into the back of the SUV and began licking Holly's ear. The little girl giggled at Friday's antics. Maddie had her out of the car and whisked her into her father's room.

"Dada snoozing. Bye-bye Dada."

Holly waved a short little arm and Maddie closed the door and had her back outside. She retrieved the car seat from the SUV and belted it into the back of the Packard before loading Holly into it. Friday jumped in back to keep Holly company.

"Hi-hi Fwiday." She reached to hug him, but not before he got a lick in. She giggled and waved and kicked her feet with joy.

I hit the button to bring down the Packard's convertible top. "You better call Angela while I get us out of here. There's no telling when the police might pounce. If they do, we'll be a long time explaining why we have a kidnapped girl in the back seat."

"Kidnap? Fwiday kidnap?"

"Oh-oh. It sounds like Holly just learned a new word, Jim."

32

Jim Nash and Maddie Spence occupied the bench in front of their upstairs office. A cool, early-evening breeze brought them out. It floated down the street, causing the leaves of the palm trees scattered along the street to make a rustling sound. It did the same to the umbrellas above the tables on the sidewalk cafés, although the sound was more akin to flapping.

Maddie's bruised head was healing slowly. The discoloration was fading, but not fast enough for her liking.

Friday sat between the couple, looking good-boy proud in the bandana around his neck. He peered out over his domain. His head turned, following and investigating people and children and dogs on leashes strolling by. He sniffed and snorted. His tail swept the sidewalk.

"I could use a cup of coffee. Jimbo. How about you? Want anything?"

Jim shook his head. "No. I'm fine."

Maddie made to head off to the coffee shop down the street at the end of the block. It was out of sight, around a corner. Friday got up, ready to accompany her. "No Friday. Stay. I'll be right back."

She looked at Jim. "I don't have the leash," she explained.

Reluctantly, Friday sat and looked urgently up at Jim, but not before making his displeasure known. He turned a circle and looked after his mistress, already half-way down the block and gaining ground fast.

"All right, Friday. I'll cover for you again. Go. Follow your mistress."

The dog woofed his gratitude and scampered off down the street. His tail was still. His tongue hung out as he raced after Maddie. He halted at the corner, looked back at Jim, and sat on his haunches.

Good boy, Friday, Jim said to no one in particular. He kept a steady gaze on the dog, knowing Friday wouldn't lose sight of his mistress. It was a couple of minutes before Friday began retracing his steps as fast as his legs would carry him.

The detective sat up, alert, wondering, and then Maddie appeared from around the corner. He witnessed her catch sight of her dog running down the sidewalk toward him. He held out his hand. It held a treat. He called to the dog. "Come on, Friday. Good boy."

Friday knew what to do. His nose nuzzled Jim's hand and came up with the treat. He gobbled it down as Jim stroked his neck.

"Very good boy. You look absolutely dashing in that bandana."

Friday sat, craned his neck up at Jim, and woofed agreement as Maddie arrived, huffing and puffing.

"All right, you two. Friday, was that you I saw high-tailing it down the street ahead of me?"

Friday looked up at Jim. The man was staring off into the distance. He was going to be no help. Instinctively, the dog knew he was on his own. He sidled up to Maddie and nosed the back of her knee. She laughed at his antics.

"Your nose is freezing, dog. And by the way, I know it

was you. I recognized the bandana."

"What was that, Maddie? Friday is a good boy. He sat with me the entire time."

Jim reached to pet Friday and managed to feed the black Lab another treat. Maddie pretended not to notice as he spoke to the dog. "Good boy, Friday."

Grinning, she handed over the coffee cup. Jim took a sip.

"You two, I swear. What am I going to do with the both of you?"

Check out all six books of the Harry Delaney Adventure series. Find out why Harry makes his way from the North African desert to the Mexican Baja. Discover how he ends up having a triumphal return to the deserts of North Africa.

Print books

Jim Nash
Jim Nash The Beginning
Gun Crazy
Gun Crazy 2
Gun Crazy 3
Fallen Angels
Last Stop to Nowhere
Revenge is Justice
Escape / Forget Me Not
Wedding Bell Blues / Breakdown
Mexico Time
No Free Ride / Gone
LOBO
Stealing America
Blame It on Djibouti
No Escape
Trouble in Paradise
Nash & Delaney Collide

Harry Delaney Adventures
Dead Reckoning
Lie Cheat Steal
Uncharted
Go-Around
Sand Storm
Harry Delaney Collection

Frank Ross Biker Tales
No Way Out
Bad Girls
Bank Robber Dames

Other
The Last President

Print books

Jim Nash
Jim Nash The Beginning
Gun Crazy
Gun Crazy 2
Gun Crazy 3
Fallen Angels
Last Stop to Nowhere
Revenge is Justice
Escape / Forget Me Not
Wedding Bell Blues / Breakdown
Mexico Time
No Free Ride / Gone
LOBO
Stealing America
Blame It on Djibouti
No Escape
Trouble in Paradise
Nash & Delaney Collide

Harry Delaney Adventures
Dead Reckoning
Lie Cheat Steal
Uncharted
Go-Around
Sand Storm
Harry Delaney Collection

Frank Ross Biker Tales
No Way Out
Bad Girls
Bank Robber Dames

Other
The Last President

About the author

Aviator. Motorcycle rider. Vagabond. Drifter. Trouble-maker. Jack of all trades and master of none. Peter has been riding and writing about the places he's been and the people he's seen for quite a few years. Some of his writing is factual; some of it isn't. He likes to leave it up to readers to decide for themselves those lies that might be the truth.

Peter Duke is a Canadian author. He resides and writes in a small college town in Southern Ontario.

https://pxduke.com

peterxduke@gmail.com

PX DUKE

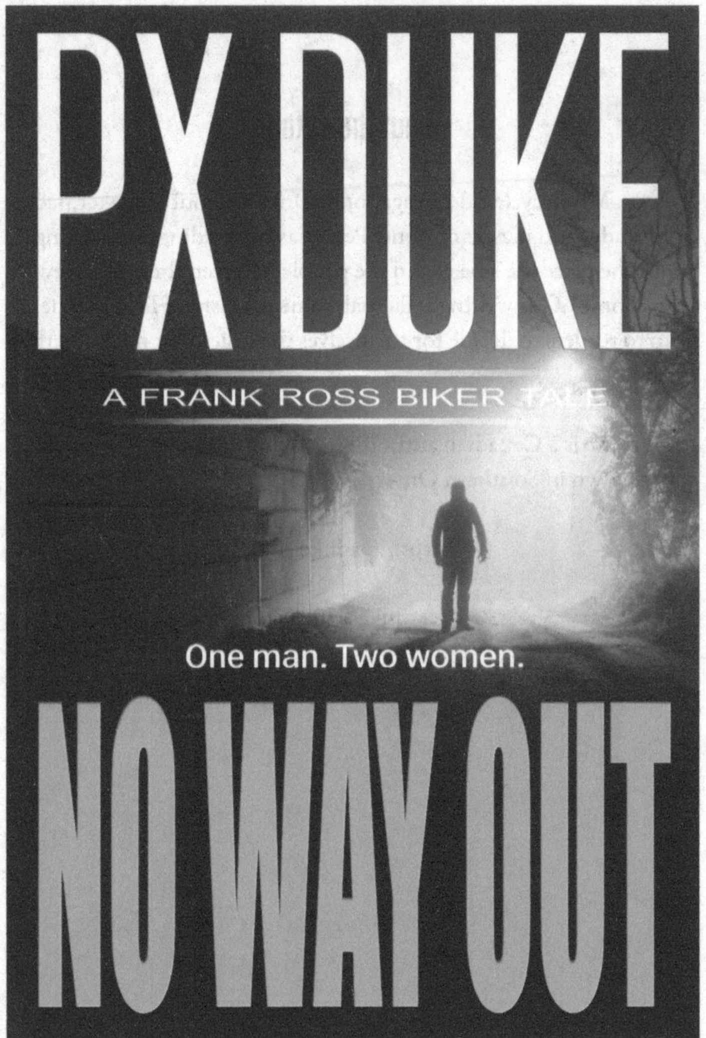

Frank Ross is out of Mexico riding north. He's just across la línea looking for shade and water. He finds it, and a lot more than he bargained for when he breaks down at a casino by the Salton Sea.

9 781928 161622